'Ever since our quarrel in the car park I had the idea you might be a fiery young woman.' Now Max's eyes sparked as he caught and held Fleur's gaze. 'You're a real little fire-cat, Fleur. Did your mother wean you on tiger's milk?'

There was a hint of humour in his last words, but it was lost on Fleur. 'Tigers have claws, you know, Max. And sometimes we use them.'

'Aha, so you're a fighting she-cat too! I've heard tell that a fighting she-cat scratches her mate's face——' Max continued provocatively slowly. 'But only in the mating season.'

With a skilful gliding movement he turned her in his arms, holding her captive and close. Then he kissed her half-open surprised mouth with passion.

Sara Burton was convent educated and trained as a physiotherapist at a school in the Midlands. She has worked in England, Scandinavia and North America and received her B.Sc. in Physical Therapy from a Western Canadian University. Currently she is engaged in independent research related to partial dislocations of joints in the lower limb. She is a bird fancier with special interest in homing pigeons.

Previous titles

HAWAIIAN HEALING
HEART SEARCHING
EXPERT TREATMENT

CAUGHT IN THE CROSSFIRE

BY

SARA BURTON

MILLS & BOON LIMITED
ETON HOUSE   18–24 PARADISE ROAD
RICHMOND   SURREY   TW9 1SR

*First published in Great Britain 1991
by Mills & Boon Limited*

© Sara Burton 1991

*Australian copyright 1991
Philippine copyright 1992
This edition 1992*

ISBN 0 263 77562 3

*Set in 11½ on 12½ pt Linotron Palatino
03-9202-40144
Typeset in Great Britain by Centracet, Cambridge
Made and printed in Great Britain*

CHAPTER ONE

ORTHOPAEDIC surgeon Max Buchanan didn't look anything like the ogre Fleur's father made him out to be. In fact he was rather handsome, if you liked those chiselled features.

Fleur eyed him over the top of her fountain pen. Unlike her final year physiotherapy classmates, she wasn't taking notes during Mr Buchanan's lecture on the biomechanics of posture. She didn't have to. She knew anatomy back to front and literally inside out, because her father was a professor of the subject at the nearby university.

Max Buchanan had commanded attention immediately he had introduced himself, and outlined his short series of evening lectures. Now, every head was raised expectantly. And this was a feat in itself, because the class was physically and mentally tired by five o'clock on Friday. They had just finished a full week of clinical placement treating patients.

His deep voice was shot through with enthusiasm. 'Bears can naturally assume an upright posture, but they can't straighten the segments of their legs like man. Man alone was proud and stood erect.'

Here's a man who's not only proud, but arrogant, thought Fleur, and she studied her lecturer critically.

He was dressed in an immaculately tailored dove-grey wool suit. The style was totally professional, but his silk feather-print tie sported a dash of cavalier colour against his cream shirt.

I bet he just loves admiring himself in the shaving mirror, she thought moodily, and began sketching the outline of a St George and a dragon.

Unconsciously she gave her St George the physical features of Max Buchanan, and the exactness of her portrait was remarkable. His intelligent half-smile, his dark short-cropped hair and glinting brown eyes were perfectly portrayed in pen and ink.

'Correct alignment of all segments of the skeleton is important. Not only does it prevent undue wear and tear on the joints, but it enhances the efficient working of the internal organs.'

He was an assured speaker, standing in front of the class with his feet wide apart. Fleur noticed that although he had come prepared with notes, he hardly consulted them. They lay static on the lectern.

'The position of the pelvis and the spine is all-important too.' Buchanan strode easily towards a skeleton that hung suspended from an iron hanger.

A cursory glance made the surgeon's straight eyebrows rise. 'Now here's a poor fellow who, no doubt, suffered in life and who'll teach us a few things.'

Everyone sat up and craned their necks. Fleur had to lean right over her best friend's desk. At this moment she wished she weren't sitting at the back.

'Yes, this fellow had a structural curve of his spine. . .a scoliosis.' Max Buchanan indicated the lateral curve of the spinal column.

Then with his index finger he pointed out the bony changes. 'Look how the bodies of the individual vertebrae have rotated.' He took great care to point out each detail, supporting and tipping the skeleton almost with reverence, almost as if the man were still alive.

'And here is the result of the deformity of the building blocks of the spine. . .a diagonal thorax.'

His fingers traced the backward bulge of the ribs on one side and the accommodating flattening on the other.

'This is a slight case,' he continued. 'But I've no doubt you all know the most famous scoliotic in literature. . . Victor Hugo's Quasimodo.'

Many of the class nodded in agreement,

and so did Fleur. The lecture was taking an interesting turn.

'That was a great tragic romance. Because the ugly bellringer of Notre Dame cathedral was capable of the most pure love for the beautiful gypsy girl Esmeralda.'

Fleur glanced around the class and every female eye was riveted; even the two male students looked captivated.

'Quasimodo was a classic example of how everybody needs someone to love.'

Here, Fleur thought, Max Buchanan paused for effect.

'I think it would be useful if I gave some lectures on sex for the disabled. . .it's surprising what questions patients ask. And you, as physios, will receive quite a few. So I hope I'll be asked back to lecture; it's an important subject.'

Clever devil, thought Fleur. Everyone will be dying to hear that! She resumed her sketching with almost angry strokes as she hatched in her St George's chain mail.

She did not see Max Buchanan turn and consult a piece of paper on the lectern.

'Who is Mrs Ros Lindy?' he asked, scanning the class quickly and letting his eye rest on Fleur's corn-coloured hair which was drawn back into a French roll.

Fleur's best friend shot up her arm and introduced herself. The surgeon's gaze shifted and there was the faintest look of relief in his eyes.

'I examined young Mikey Lockett in clinic this afternoon, Mrs Lindy. And I must say I was impressed by your treatment.'

Ros almost purred out loud after this unexpected praise, and Fleur was pleased for her friend, because the twelve-year-old patient was a bit of a cheeky monster, and reinforcing the importance of his home exercise régime had been quite a task.

Max Buchanan explained to the class in general. 'Mikey is a scoliotic in a Milwaukee brace, but I hope his curve—unlike Quasimodo's very severe one—will be brought under control by effective team treatment.'

Ros was in a state of euphoria from that moment on, but Fleur's vicarious pleasure was to be terminated immediately. Max Buchanan had come to the part of his lecture that would make her very angry.

'Studying the literature suggests that a parallel position of the feet is the best alignment for the relaxed standing posture of man, when the feet are placed together. This rationale relates to the mechanisms of the foot, and to its relationship to other joints in the leg.'

Fleur gritted her teeth.

Max Buchanan continued, 'Some authorities believe that a certain amount of out-toeing is correct for standing and walking. But from an

orthopaedic surgeon's point of view this out-
toeing might result in weakening of the structures of the foot.'

Staring steadfastly at the tip of her pen,
Fleur could not bring herself to look up. This
was the ongoing academic argument between
her father and Max Buchanan.

Professor Villiers had two passions in life.
One was Fleur's mother, and the other was
the biomechanics of the foot, particularly in
relation to the standard standing posture.

Sadly, Fleur's mother had died a year ago,
and her father had coped by throwing all his
energies into his university work. This might
have been a lasting help to the Professor, had
it not been for the fact that he was about to
retire. But unfortunately he had got the idea
into his head that when you retired life
stopped, because you were of no further use
to society.

Her father's state of health worried Fleur
terribly. And the situation had been made
worse by the public argument, which had
taken the form of letters published in the
medical journals.

Basically Fleur's father believed that the toes
should point slighly outwards at an angle of
between thirty and forty degrees. Like other
authorities, he believed that this gave good
balance to the lateral stability of the human
frame.

There were, in actual fact, good and valid arguments for both toes pointing forwards and toes pointing slightly out to the side. But the facts had never been empirically substantiated by research. And so the old wrangle rumbled on and on.

It was ironic that Max Buchanan should have been invited to lecture Fleur's class on this precise topic. Being new to this area health authority in the Midlands he had no idea, as yet, of her true identity.

Fleur could hear her lecturer setting out the arguments. And if she had been objective she might have given him credit for airing both sides of the argument.

But after a while she was lost to the sound of his cool, rational voice. All she was thinking about was the problem of her father. So she concentrated on her sketch, filling in the scales on the body of her dragon.

She was so absorbed that she was no longer aware that Max Buchanan had left his position at the front of the class. And when Ros gave a stifled cough as a warning it was too late.

A pair of large capable hands swept noiselessly across her desk, brushing her hand and pen to one side. Then in an instant they had captured her file full of electrotherapy notes and the offending portrait.

Her heart began to beat wildly and she expected an immediate rebuke. But Max Buchanan had concealed her file beneath a wad of his own lecture notes. And now he continued his talk as if nothing surprising or suspicious had happened.

This state of suspended animation shocked and numbed all her nerve-endings. She was only just aware of Ros pushing a sheet of blank paper in front of her.

Ros mumbled, 'Take notes. Act like Buchanan. Act as if nothing has happened.'

Mechanically Fleur tried to do just that, and her pen flew across the page, taking down his words verbatim.

In one respect she was lucky, because the lecture was about to end. But there was another bombshell in store for her.

Max Buchanan's voice was a master of concealment. 'Mrs Wright, the head of your school, has asked me to set you a small task. Submit a ten-page essay to me this time next week. The topic is the position of the foot in the relaxed standing posture.'

Fleur could hardly believe her ears. Fate was conspiring against her. The rest of the class moaned at the idea of more work on top of their study load for their finals.

Looking straight into Fleur's eyes, Max Buchanan said, 'I want this essay to take the form of a search of the literature. Take great care to mention all your references.'

With a curt nod, he thanked the class for

their attention and saying, 'Good evening,' swept up all his papers and strode out of the class.

'Quick!' urged Ros. 'Follow him. Apologise, but get your notes back. You know you'll need them.'

Fleur sighed. She didn't want a confrontation, especially with this man. 'I'm not going to enjoy this,' she replied, then ran down the two flights of stairs of the Edwardian building and out into the warm spring sunshine.

Halfway across the car park she spotted Max Buchanan striding away at great speed. If she didn't hurry he'd be across that road and soon he'd be lost in the complex of the General Hospital.

A few yards behind him she called his name. But to her annoyance he neither broke his stride nor turned to acknowledge her. She was forced to run round him and stand in his path.

'Excuse me, Mr Buchanan,' she started more humbly this time. 'I'm sorry if I offended you by not taking notes during your lecture. I was concentrating and listening. . .really.'

He made himself deliberately taller by straightening out his spine and, peering down at her through his sooty black eyelashes, he spoke coldly. 'Do you have some great evolutionary advantage inside your brain, young lady? Have you got a video lodged there? And can you push a button on the side of your head and play back the sound of my words, and the diagrams that I drew on the board?'

Fleur was nonplussed and she stood momentarily wavering in front of him. Some sort of an explanation was called for now. And she was going to be hard pressed not to reveal the whole truth.

'Before I started my physio training I took a science degree, I studied anatomy. . .' Here she paused to consider. 'And I did some research on the foot.'

'Ah. . .' he said, subduing his tone a shade. 'That explains why you're a little bit older than the majority of your classmates.'

She nodded but said nothing. He must be mentally working out that she was twenty-four. But she didn't want to give him any more concrete information about her identity. A soft blush stole up her neck as she felt him scrutinise her face.

'Being that little bit older will help you when you're treating my patients.'

She thought his tone was sincere, and it made her feel on edge for some reason.

He continued, 'You'll have had more experience of life, and the patients will appreciate this. They're more likely to believe that you know what you're talking about.'

'I hope so,' she replied guardedly. Then,

after an awkward silence, 'May I have my notes back, please?'

'If they're all on anatomy, then you won't need them, will you?' His eyes were teasing.

She felt herself tense. 'They're on electrotherapy. They're about laser treatment, ultrasound, and short-wave diathermy.'

'I ought to read up on those treatments myself,' he replied. 'After all, I should know exactly what I'm sending my patients for.'

Was he ever going to give those wretched notes back? This altercation was going on far too long for Fleur.

Sensing her discomfort, he shuffled her file to the top of his papers. And, glancing at the front cover, he read her name out loud with surprise. 'Fleur Villiers. . .' His eyebrows shot up.

Now the cat was out of the bag.

'Villiers,' he repeated. 'You have a very eminent name in anatomy circles.'

Her sapphire eyes darkened. 'My father is Professor David Villiers.' She spoke the name with pride, as if offering Max Buchanan some challenge.

'Is he indeed! No wonder you know all about anatomy, and especially the foot.' His smile was broad, showing his brilliant white teeth. 'I expect you've had some lessons on the subject ever since you were a little girl.

And every time you had a pork chop or a leg of lamb on the dining-room table.'

Fleur was miffed that Max Buchanan should have guessed so accurately exactly what meal-times had been like in her family. At one point her mother had wished they had been vegetarian!

Fortunately Max Buchanan didn't wait for an answer and carried on enthusiastically, 'Your father and I are currently having a lively discussion in the *Anatomy Journal*.'

'I know,' she broke in vehemently. 'I'm fully aware of the war with words that you're fighting with my father.'

This defensive outburst seemed to shock him, and he replied in the gentlest of voices, 'In science, and particularly medical science, it's best to think that nothing is permanently or fully understood. Arguments should be brought out into the open. The *Journal* is the best place to air them. It can only lead to more concrete knowledge.'

They had got to the very crux of the matter, something that Fleur wanted to avoid. But they were in the midst of it now. And she was going to say her piece.

'Just because somebody holds an opinion that's old, it doesn't necessarily mean that it's wrong. Take Leonardo da Vinci's work on the principles of posture in his *Treatise on*

Painting—those principles have never been refuted.'

Max Buchanan's dark eyes sparkled with delight. 'I see you can argue intelligently and *passionately*, Miss Villiers. I like that. And those are two qualities that a good researcher should possess.'

Fleur felt she was on dangerous ground. There was something magnetic about this man. 'Please may I have my notes back?' she repeated.

He flipped open the cover and stared at her drawing. 'This work is particularly fine. Have you studied portraiture at art school? This fellow is very handsome. I can see the likeness quite easily.' He stroked his thumb down his jaw line.

Conceited swine, thought Fleur. Fancy thinking I was putting his portrait in the St George!

Her reply was more of a reflex. 'Oh yes, sir, I was taking the portrait from life when I did the dragon's head.'

He gave a deep-throated chuckle, then met her eyes with no malice. His next words were carefully chosen. 'You haven't drawn the princess. Your picture isn't complete.'

'She doesn't figure in this scene,' she replied emphatically.

His eyes crinkled in a most attractive way. 'I wouldn't say that.' Then after a short pause he continued, 'How about a bit of bartering? If I can keep the picture, you can have your notes.'

This wasn't to Fleur's liking at all. The surgeon's whole attitude disturbed her in a deep way. 'That's fine by me,' she answered cautiously, and held out her hand.

He unclipped her drawing and gave back her file.

To make a quick exit she spoke rapidly. 'Thank you, Mr Buchanan. Goodbye.' And turning, she was about to retreat when he called softly after her.

'Goodbye, Miss Villiers. I'll look forward to reading your essay. I'm sure it'll give me great pleasure.'

Fleur halted in her tracks and swung round. It infuriated her that anything she did would cause him the least pleasure. 'Good afternoon again, Mr Buchanan,' she said curtly. How was she going to get around that essay? She hadn't worked that out yet!

Fleur walked the long way home in order to clear her mind and reflect. Ros had been waiting for her, and had pulled her into an empty massage-room in order to hear about the scene in the car park.

Ros was a mature student of forty. She had had her family when she was young, and now her two boys were away at college. Fleur respected her opinion and often confided in her.

But on this occasion she couldn't agree with her friend. Ros believed that Max Buchanan was smitten with Fleur. And if she wanted to stop the academic argument in the journals, she ought to encourage the relationship with the surgeon. If they knew each other more intimately, it would be easy to influence him. But this idea was repugnant to Fleur.

Sitting in the lounge of her old family house now, Fleur found it difficult to concentrate on her studies.

Although she had lived away from home since the time she had entered university, she had wanted to return following her mother's death. Her father had been against the idea, saying that she should live her own life. But when Fleur insisted he had put up no argument, and she felt that secretly he was pleased.

Professor Villiers entered the house as the dusk was falling. Fleur was shocked to see that his face was more gaunt than usual, and the dark circles under his eyes blue-black.

After she had fetched him some hot coffee he sat in his wing-back chair in the lounge and told her the problem.

Producing the anatomy journal from his briefcase, he began, 'Listen to this letter from that young upstart Buchanan!'

Fleur gritted her teeth.

'Everything he writes is full of academic venom. And an intentional smear on my work.' The Professor read aloud, '"A confident explanation, but one not founded on fact, or experimental science." And here, "Opinions that remain as yet unconfirmed".'

Covering her face with her hand, Fleur listened resignedly.

'Hostility and envy lurk around every corner.' Her father slumped back in his chair.

'Oh, that sounds just like him, Dad!' Fleur replied furiously. 'He sounds exactly like that in real life. In fact, he delivered his lecture this evening on those same arrogant lines.'

Immediately she had let this out she could have bitten her tongue.

Professor Villiers screwed up his face. 'I thought you had that lecture on the principles of posture this evening,' he said.

Fleur groaned inwardly. She had meant to keep this from him. 'Mrs Wright, our head, had a difficult time trying to find a replacement for you. Mr Buchanan only stepped in at the last minute.'

Her father's protracted sigh caused her some anguish. 'After all, Dad, you did back out because you said you were so overworked this year,' she added.

After a pause, her father said, 'Well, I've

got an ace up my sleeve, Fleur. You old dad isn't beaten yet.'

She leaned forward expectantly.

'The only way to settle this running controversy once and for all is to do some proper research. This will unequivocally support my work.'

'Brilliant idea, but where are you going to get the funds?' she asked.

'The University, of course. There's a two-year grant coming up. I'm going to write up and submit a research proposal. I'm going to start that tonight.'

'I wish you all the luck in the world.' Fleur turned her face away. It was highly unlikely that the old Professor would be given the money. Usually it went to the more junior staff. This would end being another blow to her father's already depleted ego.

'I intend to expose this Buchanan's muddled thinking,' her father continued, a note of purpose in his voice now, 'and I've heard that many in the medical world wonder at his credulity. He's known as the "music doctor", you know.'

'Why?' Fleur asked curiously.

'He's not a science man through and through. He trained at the Royal Academy of Music before entering medicine. I can't help thinking his logic must be suspect.' He drummed his fingers. 'Either you're a science or you're an arts man.'

Later on that night as Fleur lay wide awake in bed she reflected on her father's arch-rival. Max Buchanan was a clever man and with a dash of brilliance about him.

He'd lectured and entertained the class exceptionally well. And he'd tried to use his winning charm on her in the car park. The best word she could think of to describe him was 'artful'.

Now the problem he posed for her father was a huge one. How were they going to win against this surgeon?

She thought long and hard into the small hours, and only then when the birds were singing the dawn chorus did she have some idea. She didn't know how they would win the big battle of the research. But she had a plan for that essay that Max Buchanan had set. And it made her giggle out loud.

CHAPTER TWO

'HAVE you any idea what this emergency meeting for the whole school is about, Ros?'

Fleur was jammed tightly against her friend in the biggest lecture-room.

Ros sounded serious. 'Whatever it is, it's mighty important. Everyone's here, even some students from the outlying hospitals.'

At that moment the deputy head, Miss Pringle, entered the room. She was followed by a very proper-looking woman in her late sixties.

'May I have everyone's attention!' Miss Pringle called above the noise.

Immediately there was silence.

Miss Pringle had taken her place at the lectern, and the elderly woman stood behind and to her side. The deputy began without preamble.

'I'm afraid I have some bad news. As you know, Mrs Wright was lecturing in Winnipeg, Canada. Unfortunately she was involved in an accident on one of the highways and has sustained multiple fractures of her legs.'

There was an audible gasp from the students, and Fleur raised her eyebrows at Ros.

'Fortunately I'm able to report that she's stable, but her injuries are severe enough to keep her away from work for several months.'

Miss Pringle drew a deep breath. 'Everyone in the school must pull together at this time of crisis. But I have some good news, particularly for you students about to take your finals.'

Turning to the elderly woman, she said, 'May I introduce Miss Majors? She has very kindly agreed to help us in our time of need.'

Everyone's eyes were riveted.

'Miss Majors used to be the head of this school some decades ago—in fact, her time here was described as notorious. She was sent here to close the school, but through sheer determination she managed to put the school back on its feet and expand it. Now, every student here is living proof of the high academic standard that we can achieve.'

There was a murmur of approval throughout the school.

'During Mrs Wright's absence, I shall be taking over the administrative work. And Miss Majors here will take some lectures, and she will also be acting as a clinical instructress for you students who are based in department at the General Hospital.'

Fleur, Ros and most of the final-year students were working in the department of the General.

Miss Pringle ended her talk by calling on

every student to give their utmost support during the time of crisis.

As the two physiotherapy teachers left the classroom Fleur spoke to Ros in a subdued tone. 'That's dreadful news about Mrs Wright.'

'Yes. I think we'd better take up a collection and send some flowers.'

Trevor, one of the male students, tapped Fleur on the shoulder. 'However old do you think Miss Majors is? She's a very proper-looking woman.'

'A hundred and one in the shade at least. But that experience might make her a first-rate teacher,' said Fleur.

Trevor didn't sound convinced. 'She might have been excellent twenty or thirty years ago, but I don't know how she'll be concerning all the modern techniques.'

But Miss Majors' first lesson came as a revelation to everybody.

As usual they were in the big massage-room, sitting at the plinths so that they could use them as desks.

Standing in front of the class with a no-nonsense look in her eyes, Miss Majors was about to start lecturing when she turned at the sound of a gentle tap on the closed door.

Trevor poked his head in and, stealing in quietly, said, 'I'm sorry I'm late.'

'What's your name, young man?' came the imperious question.

'Trevor Link.'

'The missing Link, I presume. Please sit down. But remember that punctuality is an all important quality in physiotherapists. . . particularly for the treatment of patients.'

Trevor turned brick red and slid quietly on to a seat next to his friend. And the rest of the class wondered what was in store.

Miss Majors began again. 'I've taken some time to observe you students in the clinical situation. The standard of your treatments is, on the whole, very high. But I feel that the basic handling of patients could improve. And so our classes from now on will include some instruction on massage.'

Fleur cupped her hand over her mouth and whispered to Ros, 'I thought massage was dropped from the syllabus ages ago.'

There was no time for more than a 'Shh. . .' from Ros before Miss Majors continued.

'Massage is one of the oldest sciences. Even the Chinese used frictions on the soft tissues of the body, and that was thousands of years before Christ.'

Everybody decided that it would be prudent to take notes.

'Massage is not the mere rubbing of the body. It requires a great deal of intelligence, and a good working knowledge of anatomy, And the good masseur should be able to establish an empathy with the patient.'

No one in the class could quarrel with that, but when they were ordered to stand at the end of the plinths Fleur, like everyone else, had grave misgivings.

Walking up and down to inspect the students, Miss Majors gave her explanation. 'Personal appearance is all-important. Everyone should take a pride in their white coat.'

Poor Trevor was singled out for another reproof. He had a button missing.

'White coats should be scrupulously clean.' The teacher indicated an ink stain below one of Fleur's pockets.

'Now, please present your hands for inspection.'

Behind Miss Majors' back, Fleur pulled a face at Ros.

Unfortunately for Ros, Miss Majors found the slightest remains of some nail varnish. 'Mrs Lindy,' she rebuked, 'nails should be innocent of scarlet polish!'

Fleur thought she was going to burst out laughing. This military-style inspection was on prehistoric lines.

The remaining time of this class was spent in a practical session. Miss Majors demonstrated the massage technique for dispersal of œdema at the ankle. This was the swelling caused by fluid in the interstitial tissues. Then the class was divided into pairs, and Ros volunteered to be the operator, while Fleur was pleased to lie back on the plinth and play the model. Like the rest of the models in the class, Fleur thought she would have a relaxing time. But this idea was abruptly brought to an end, as Miss Majors continually asked questions about anatomy and pathology.

By the time the class ended everyone was exhausted, and glad to see the back of their new teacher.

Trevor, who naturally played the part of a clown, and who would have been just as at home in a three-ring circus, rapped on an arm table and called for attention.

Marching military style up and down between the plinths, he mimicked Miss Majors' voice. 'A good physiotherapist always remembers names correctly. And my name is Miss Sergeant Majors!' He gave an exaggerated salute to the class, and they all fell about laughing.

Some of the tension had been dispelled, but Trevor brought up a more serious concern. 'I don't know when I'm ever going to use this old-fashioned massage. I would have thought that the Jobst intermittent positive pressure machine, and active exercises in elevation,

were the modern treatments for an œdematous ankle.'

Fleur swung her legs over the side of the
plinth and sat up. 'Don't worry, Trev, you'll
be using these ancient techniques every day
when you're qualified. As long as you get a
job on Noah's ark!'

Again there was hilarious laughter, and Ros
unsuccessfully tried to use her admonishing
voice to tell everyone to give Miss Majors a
chance. But she had no effect because she was
giggling too much herself.

Miss Majors posed one problem. But to
Fleur, Max Buchanan was a far more dangerous one.

As his Friday evening lecture approached,
she felt a flutter of excitement mounting
throughout her body. She had calculated long
and hard about his set essay for the position
of the foot in the relaxed standing posture.
Now she was sure that her tactics would win.

Fortunately, Mr Buchanan's second lecture
dealt with sections of the body well away from
the foot, so Fleur had no problems concentrating while she took notes.

The early evening sun was blisteringly hot,
and Max Buchanan had taken off his jacket.
Fleur was impressed to see that the jacket had
not been padded at the shoulders; his own
deltoid muscles gave that impressive width.

While he was writing on the board, she had

to admit that his torso was magnificently sculptured. That clear definition of muscle moving beneath his white shirt must have been acquired by physical exercise. No doubt he lifted weights to keep in shape.

Fleur's tension and excitement began to mount as the lesson drew to an end.

Max Buchanan ordered, 'Hand in your essays as you leave the room.'

Ros bent close to Fleur's ear and whispered, 'You can't seriously give that in to the man!'

'Just you watch me!' replied Fleur haughtily.

'Well, I think it's a terribly childish game you're playing. And one that won't help your father one jot.'

Fleur shrugged her shoulders. And as she had planned, she sat at the back of the class and waited until everyone else had filed out.

She knew that Max Buchanan was aware of her, because he casually glanced up in her direction, as he shuffled his papers.

Then, with as much poise as she could muster, she walked towards him and presented her work.

'Thank you, Miss Villiers,' he began with a broad smile. 'I've been looking forward——' His words came to an abrupt halt. Then he looked at her with a steely candour, his brown eyes burning into hers like lasers. 'And is this the sum total of your effort?'

'Yes,' she replied with icy correctness. She

could feel her chest becoming tighter and her breathing more rapid and shallow as he surveyed the blank piece of paper with a barely concealed smouldering anger.

'A cursory glance shows me you've made two mistakes. You haven't dated or put your name to this.'

Looking up at him with steadfast eyes that betrayed her discomfort, Fleur began to feel her pulse race. 'I suppose my mind went a blank.'

'Obviously!' Then after narrowing his eyes he said, 'Very well, Miss Villiers, have it your own way.' His voice was curt as he swept up his papers and strode towards the door.

Then, turning, he faced her square on. There was a significant stillness about his whole body, and when he spoke he chose his words carefully, so that they hit Fleur like a volley of arrowheads.

'I shall mark these essays as soon as possible. My secretary will type up the results. And, like my medical students' results, I shall have them posted on your bulletin board so that the whole School of Physiotherapy can view them. Goodnight, Miss Villiers.'

Fleur stood stunned and motionless. Her strategy had failed catastrophically. It had been short-sighted, because she had thought no further than seeing the astonishment on

Max Buchanan's face as she handed in the paper.

Undoubtedly she had been acting entirely on her emotions. From now on her tactics had better be more sophisticated. If she didn't pull herself together, he would win the big battle over her father hands down!

Early on Monday morning Fleur was working in the physiotherapy department of the General. She was tidying away a short-wave diathermy machine following the treatment of a patient when she heard Miss Majors call her name.

'Ah, here you are. I believe you're treating Mrs Oliver.'

'Yes,' replied Fleur. 'She's due for an appointment any time now.'

Consulting a notepad, Miss Majors interrupted. 'Her son is having trouble with his car, so he won't be able to bring her today. He's cancelled the appointment. But as you're at a loose end, and one of the qualifieds has been summoned to an emergency on the wards, I've arranged an interesting alternative for you.'

How interesting was this alternative going to be? thought Fleur. Was she about to be assigned to clear out the gym equipment cupboard?

'I'd like you to help Mr Buchanan in his clinic.'

You could have knocked Fleur down with a feather. She hadn't expected a meeting with the surgeon so soon. And she had been pondering over the idea of writing up his essay, so that she could get some sort of a mark. But she had done nothing about it.

Reluctantly she followed Miss Majors into the little clinic area that was situated next door.

'I've brought Miss Villiers to assist you, Mr Buchanan,' said Miss Majors. 'I thought she'd be of help.'

The surgeon swivelled round on his captain's chair. He had been reading a pile of patient notes. Then, leaning back, he surveyed Fleur with a gleam in his eye.

'Excellent, Miss Majors. Because the next patient I'm about to examine might prove to be ideal for a student, as long as it turns out to be osteo-arthritis of the lumbar spine, and nothing more sinister.'

Miss Majors looked delighted. 'That sounds just the ticket. And I'm sure Miss Villiers will be pleased to accept any individual tuition on the subject.'

'That's exactly what I had in mind.' He stood up and ushered the teacher out of the room.

He looks far too pleased about this chance

meeting, thought Fleur. I wonder what's in that devious mind now?

Max Buchanan launched straight into information about his next patient. 'Mrs Violet Jolley is sixty-nine and has had no significant disease in her life. While I read up her X-ray reports could you check that she's adequately undressed for my examination.'

'Of course.'

'The other week I examined an old lady of eighty who wore a real whalebone corset. It took the nurse and me a full ten minutes to unlace her!'

'All right,' laughed Fleur, and left.

When she entered the examination cubicle she was confronted by an elderly lady sitting on the side of the high plinth, and a younger woman very expensively dressed.

Fleur introduced herself and said, 'I'm sorry, Mrs Jolley, but you'll have to take that straw hat off, because the surgeon will want you to lie flat.'

'Certainly, my dear,' came the amiable reply, and she lifted off the hat that had been sitting at a very jaunty angle.

The younger woman, who Fleur guessed was in her forties, took the hat and spoke in an affected voice full of glottal stops. 'Will we have to wait much longer? It was difficult enough getting a parking space here, and I've still got to get a pile of shopping from town.'

'Mr Buchanan will be with your mother as soon as possible.'

As Fleur was closing the door to the examination cubicle she heard, 'Really, Mother. . . This room is barely adequate, I knew we should have gone privately.'

Max Buchanan was studying back X-rays that he had slotted in the viewer. 'Look at these films,' he said.

Fleur was pleased at the idea of having the pathology explained, and she went forward eagerly.

'As long as I find nothing more on the clinical examination, it looks as if this lady's problem is simply old age. Wear and tear in her lumbar spine.'

Fleur peered at the side view of the vertebral bodies.

With the point of his Biro Max Buchanan indicated the central joints, those between the bodies of the vertebrae. 'This part of the lumbar spine is usually affected first. Look at the degeneration here, and the subsequent narrowing of the discs between the vertebral bodies.'

It was quite clear, and Fleur could see an excess of bone at the margins of the joints. 'Are these the osteophytes?' she asked, pointing out some bobbly bits with her fingertip.

'Yes. But fortunately they're not encroaching on the intervertebral foramen—these holes at the side between the vertebral bodies—and therefore I don't think they're in a position to upset the nerves from the spinal cord. That could cause exasperating pain.'

Fleur was fascinated.

Max Buchanan continued, 'These osteophytes are often beneficial, and can prevent pain later in life. We can see here that they've appeared on the lateral or outer side of the joint where the disc is weakest.'

'The body can be very clever,' marvelled Fleur.

'It certainly is,' the surgeon agreed. 'Osteophytes can play a great role in Mother Nature's self-care programme. Studies of X-rays show that by the time the patient is fifty they're in the lumbar region of ninety per cent of normal men. And at the age of sixty-five they're present in eighty per cent of normal women. They can prevent the disc from protruding and causing problems.'

Max Buchanan paused and smiled. 'Often these bony outgrowths don't cause any pain or problem. When I was a student and worked in the docklands in London, I treated many middle-aged dockers.'

Fleur was intrigued to hear him talk; he was obviously deeply committed to his work.

'The men would come for problems with other conditions, for example stones in the kidney, and I'd see on X-ray that a lot of osteophytes were in the lumbar spine. But the men still swore they had no back trouble.'

Replacing the film in its folder, he said, 'Now let's do the clinical exam and see if Mrs Jolley is a suitable patient for physio.'

Immediately they entered the cubicle the younger woman stepped forward briskly and introduced herself. 'My name is Mrs Highbrown-Clack. My husband is a partner at Highbrown-Clack and Muggles, the solicitors in the Promenade. I hope you're going to be able to help my mother.'

But Max Buchanan gave no reaction to this power play. He answered quite naturally, 'We'll do our best, of course.'

This seemed to peeve Mrs Highbrown-Clack, and she fidgeted in the background.

Max Buchanan's examination of the elderly lady was thorough and considerate. Fleur wondered at his expertise, because he didn't pull Mrs Jolley about more than was necessary.

Sitting on the edge of the plinth, he asked pertinent questions.

'It really only bothers me after a bout of gardening,' Mrs Jolley confided. 'In fact, it's quiet at the moment, as I've been resting.'

'There's nothing sinister for you to worry about.' Max Buchanan turned to include the daughter. 'I'm afraid it's just a case of normal wear and tear at the joints. And at your age,' he lowered his voice, 'I think you should expect a little aching.'

'Ah,' replied the old lady, 'that's just what I thought, nothing can be done.'

'You're right, Mrs Jolley,' he said softly. 'Nothing can reverse the wear and tear, but I'd like to send you for some physio so that you can learn how to prevent further problems.'

Mrs Jolley beamed with approval.

Then, turning to Fleur, Max Buchanan said, 'Miss Villiers here will be treating you.'

This idea was too much for Mrs Highbrown-Clack. She spoke up in a high-pitched voice. 'I'm sorry, Mr Buchanan, I simply can't allow a *student* to treat my mother.' She had obviously read Fleur's name tag.

And Fleur was shocked and not a little hurt by this outburst.

But Max Buchanan came to her aid immediately. 'Mrs Highbrown-Clack——' his tone was quiet, but full of authority '—Miss Villiers is a final-year student. It's merely a matter of weeks before she becomes qualified. Apart from that, all patients treated by students are supervised by a clinical instructor.'

Fleur could see the daughter wither under this reply.

Max Buchanan had not finished, though. 'I would gladly let Miss Villiers treat *my* mother. Not only does she have a degree in anatomy, but her father is an eminent professor in the field. So in my opinion you couldn't get better treatment in Harley Street.'

His defence had an immediate result. Mrs Highbrown-Clack simpered, 'Oh, I didn't know all that. You'll be very pleased with Miss Villiers, won't you, Mother?'

Mrs Jolley nodded timidly.

With that score settled, Max Buchanan left Fleur to arrange an appointment. And this was easily done.

Returning to him, Fleur said, 'Thank you for sticking up for me.'

He looked at her with smiling steadfast eyes. 'I spoke on the facts. And I believe you won't let me down, Fleur.'

Hearing him speak her name so softly like that, Fleur accepted it naturally. His eyes were bright and so intense that she felt something deep inside her was affected. Locked in his warm gaze, she felt her senses begin to stir in an unfamiliar way. No other man had ever affected her like this. The feeling was so strong and compelling, it was as if they were in their own little world.

Dragging her mind back to the patient, she said, 'I'll do my best with Mrs Jolley. I don't think she'll be difficult.'

A glimmer of a twinkle lit Max Buchanan's eyes, and he bent down to retrieve something from his briefcase. Pulling out a thin strip of paper, he said, 'I expect your classmates would like to know the results of my set essay on the foot.' He held the paper towards her.

Fleur's heart sank as she took it. Then, scanning the paper for her name, she gasped. She had expected to see the word 'Fail' printed boldly alongside her name. Instead she read the word 'Distinction'.

'Distinction!' she exclaimed. 'But how?'

His grin was wide and very attractive. 'I marked you on your viva voce performance in the car park. I think that told me everything I needed to know.'

She smiled with relief and met his brilliant eyes. He was having that strange but delicious effect on her again. She would have said something but for the interruption.

Miss Majors tapped on the door and announced that the qualified was back from the ward, and that now Miss Villiers was needed for her next patient.

Fleur thanked and left Max Buchanan. As she walked away to organise the treatment of her next patient, her mind was locked on the orthopaedic surgeon. If only there weren't this running battle concerning her father, then things might be very different. She would be free to get to know Max Buchanan better. And she wanted to know him a great deal better.

CHAPTER THREE

'REALLY, Mr Link, I thought I was in the gym of St Hopeless's Hospital when I was watching you take that mens' early knee class!'

Fleur was about to ask Miss Majors a question about Mrs Jolley's treatment. But, hearing this conversation from the clinical instructor's office, she backtracked a few paces out of view.

This office was situated at the end of the section in the department that contained the treatment cubicles. And because the day was hot and the office didn't have a window, the door had been left wide open.

Fleur could hear poor Trevor undergoing a debriefing. And by the sound of it he hadn't measured up.

After a few minutes he emerged with a glum face and with his head down. Fleur caught his arm and pulled him to one side.

'It can't have been that bad, Trev,' she consoled.

'Worse,' he replied, lifting the end of his tie in the air, and leaning his head to one side he gave the impression that he had been hanged.

Fleur pulled his arm down quickly. 'For

goodness' sake stop mucking about, Trev! If Miss Majors catches you, you really will be a dead man.'

'She hasn't finished with me,' he muttered. 'I've got to go back later so that she can explain more about structuring gym classes. But apparently I'm not beyond redemption.' He gave a forced smile. 'She thinks she can teach me how to have eyes in the back of my head!'

'What for?' asked Fleur, grinning back at him.

'I wasn't checking that everyone was doing their exercises properly. And at one point Miss Majors said that a patient at the back of the class was getting more exercise chewing his gum than doing his straight leg raises.'

They both giggled at this. But then Miss Majors emerged from her office and Trevor scooted off.

Putting on a suitably serious look, Fleur addressed the clinical instructor. 'Excuse me, Miss Majors, Mr Buchanan has asked for a heat treatment for Mrs Jolley's back. But he hasn't specified which type.'

Miss Majors took the requisition form and studied it. 'Ah, yes, that lady that you saw in the clinic. . .now I remember. Let's go and have a look at her, then.'

Fleur had helped Mrs Jolley to undress, and had left her lying safely on the plinth. When they drew back the cubicle curtains, they saw her quietly snoozing.

Miss Majors smiled. 'If your patient falls asleep this easily amid all the noise of a busy department, I think short-wave diathermy is out of the question as a heat treatment.'

Fleur nodded.

'If Mrs Jolley falls asleep while under the short wave she might easily move and receive a burn without knowing, until it's too late. And I don't think you, Miss Villiers, want a law-suit on your hands.'

'No, thanks,' agreed Fleur.

'I think a hot pack is the treatment of preference in this case. And assuming she can lie comfortably in any position, what position would you choose, Miss Villiers?'

It was question time for Fleur, and she thought carefully before answering. 'Side lying, because if she lies on her back and falls asleep the problem of a burn could come up again. The pressure of her body weight might impede the circulation of the blood. And if the blood isn't moving adequately to disperse the build-up of heat, the burn could occur.'

'Exactly. Good thinking. Have you completed your initial assessment?'

'Yes, and I've completed the thermal appreciation test. Mrs Jolley could tell the difference between the hot and cold test tubes.

If she's awake, she'll know if the hot pack is too hot.'

Miss Majors nodded approvingly. 'If I were you, I'd concentrate on teaching her one exercise today. With this experience being so new, it might be better to make sure she understands one exercise well, rather than go home and do several wrongly.'

Exactly as Fleur had anticipated, Mrs Jolley proved to be a co-operative and easy patient to treat. She mastered her pelvic tilt exercises with no problems, and Fleur thought she detected the ghost of a smile flicker on the elderly lady's lips.

Following the treatment, she escorted her patient to the waiting area, where they found her daughter.

'Thank you so much, Miss Villiers,' Mrs Highbrown-Clack began. 'I'm sure you've looked after my mother very well.'

'It was a pleasure,' replied Fleur naturally, slightly resenting the patronising tone.

After agreeing on the time of the next appointment Mrs Highbrown-Clack said, 'This is really working out very well. I've been able to do a lot of shopping. The stores aren't so crowded at this time.'

As Fleur watched them walk out, she had the distinct feeling that although Mrs Jolley was so accommodating, so polite, almost timid at times, there was still that air of independence, almost defiance in the way she wore her straw sun-hat.

There was a very large U-shaped desk at the end of the students' treatment area, where they could sit and write up their notes. It was next to the treatment cubicles, and any conversation could easily be overheard.

Sitting next to Trev, Fleur was writing up her notes on Mrs Jolley when she heard Ros talking to Pete Lowe.

Pete was thirty-five, a time of life when a man should be in his prime. But Pete had contracted rheumatoid arthritis when he was a teenager, and the disease had been long-standing and therefore resulted in a great deal of residual joint damage,

Listening to Ros treating Pete, Fleur reflected how unfair this disease was. The exact cause of rheumatoid arthritis remained unknown, and there were no preventive or curative treatments. And it was a systemic disease that involved organs such as the heart and lungs, as well as the joints.

Pete had a reputation for being difficult to treat. He was often cranky, owing to the excessive pain and disability. But, fortunately for Ros, he had taken a great liking to her.

He had undergone many joint replacements, and now Ros was treating his foot following some surgery at his subtalar joint— the joint below the ankle joint.

Talking to Ros, Pete sounded wearily depressed. 'I'm fed up today. I hardly had a wink of sleep last night, and ever since this morning I've been stiffer and more painful than ever.'

Ros's disembodied voice floated through the partitioning curtains. 'Do you think you were lying awkwardly in bed?'

'No,' sighed Pete. 'All I know is that I was awake so long, I hardly had a chance to let my joints rest. And now this swelling at the ankle. . .well, it's really getting me down.'

Fleur heard Ros telling him that she would fetch Miss Majors and she would take a look.

'I hope she knows what she's doing,' Pete replied languidly.

Ros reassured him, 'She's very experienced.'

Some time later, when Fleur had finished writing up Mrs Jolley's assessment and treatment notes, Ros appeared.

'Miss Majors is about to demonstrate a massage technique on Pete's ankle. Would you and Trev like to watch?' she asked.

Trevor pulled a face, but Fleur, knowing their voices could be overheard, replied brightly, 'Yes, we'd love to come.'

In the cubicle Miss Majors spoke softly to Pete. 'Do you mind acting as a demonstration model?' she asked.

'It's fine by me.' He seemed a little brighter

now. Obviously he had taken to the older clinical instructor.

Miss Majors squeezed some massage cream between her hands. 'This cream will be particularly effective for Pete, because it will improve the condition of his dry skin.'

Her patient nodded approvingly.

She used an effleurage stroke to the whole limb to begin with. This was a stroking manipulation towards the heart. After dispersing the œdema higher up the leg, she began her massage of the foot.

'Here I'm using a kneading technique,' she explained, as she worked on the anterior and posterior aspect of his foot.

'That swelling is disappearing like magic under your hands!' exclaimed Pete. He looked really pleased now.

Fleur couldn't help contrasting Pete's body with Max Buchanan's. The two men must be about the same age, but Pete's body was wasted and emaciated by the relentless disease process, while Max Buchanan had a Michelangelo-sculpted body bursting with energy.

If Pete had a body like Max Buchanan, then no doubt he wouldn't be so depressed all the time.

Miss Majors watched and gave instructions as Ros completed the massage manipulation.

'It looks more like a real foot now.' Pete was

beaming with pleasure. 'I woke up this morning feeling like a washed-up jellyfish, but now I feel a million times better!'

'Are your sleeping patterns always bad, Pete?' Miss Majors enquired.

'Dreadful!'

The clinical instructor explained, 'It's been scientifically recorded that this lack of non-restorative sleep can have a debilitating effect.'

Everyone looked intrigued.

'Yes, some studies show that there's an overnight increase of stiffness in muscles and joints. Also an increase in generalised pain and fatigue, and the feeling of being emotionally distressed.'

Pete nodded vigorously to all this.

'Rheumatoid patients feel these symptoms very badly first thing in the morning. And it's been shown that there's a specific alpha 7–11.5 Hz electro-encephalogram non-rapid eye movement sleep disturbance related to this.'

'Sounds a mouthful to me,' interrupted Pete.

Miss Majors agreed, then continued, 'One research programme used normal sedentary subjects and subjected them to noise-induced stage four non-rapid eye movement sleep disturbance, and they found a similar alpha EEG sleep pattern could be artifically induced in them. And those subjects all experienced the same musculo-skeletal and mood disturbance effects.'

'Beats me how anyone ever volunteers for these research programmes!' Pete raised his eyebrows. Everyone laughed.

'They use medical and physio students most of the time,' Miss Majors explained.

After this lecture demonstration the students all admitted that they'd been impressed. Even Trevor agreed that massage had its place.

A few afternoons later, as the students were filing out of the department at the end of the day, Miss Majors called Fleur back to her office.

'Do you live anywhere near Dolphin Road, Miss Villiers?' she asked.

'Yes, it's only a block from my house.' Fleur wondered what was coming next.

The older woman looked slightly relieved. 'I promised to deliver an electrotherapy book to one of the doctors, but I'd quite forgotten that this was my evening to work with the CP children at the Barnes Centre.'

'It won't be a problem,' said Fleur. 'I'll deliver it for you. Who's it for?'

'Mr Buchanan lives at number sixty-two Dolphin Road.'

Fleur felt her heart skip a beat. This might prove to be a good turn of fate. She had been thinking of Ros's strategy, and if she did get to know Max Buchanan better she was sure she could at least get somewhere dampening down the wrangle with her father.

Miss Majors thanked Fleur effusively, and when Fleur had changed into a pair of blue jeans and a cotton top she set off for the surgeon's house.

Number sixty-two Dolphin Road was a Victorian villa, set back from the road behind a tall verdant hedge. Climbing the flight of front stone steps, Fleur admired the elegant black iron railings. Then the front door opened and a wiry little woman of about forty deposited two empty milk bottles in the porch.

'Hello, my dear. I'm Mr Buchanan's housekeeper. May I help you?'

Fleur introduced herself. 'One of our teachers at the School of Physiotherapy has sent a textbook,' she explained.

The little woman eyed her quite openly, then said, 'Come in, my dear. Mr Buchanan is very particular about his medical stuff. He wants everything put immediately on his desk.'

She led the way into a spacious hall, and through into a study. It was a room with a high ceiling elegantly moulded. The window was big, but the desk even bigger. The top of this desk was hardly visible. It was covered haphazardly with books, journals and loose paper.

Taking the book, the housekeeper placed it in the centre of the desk, and as she did so she knocked a pile of papers to the floor.

Automatically Fleur knelt down to pick them up. But one piece of paper instantly struck a note of discord within her heart. It was dated only yesterday, and was addressed to the editor of a medical journal—the very journal in which Max Buchanan and her father were having their academic row.

The housekeeper was on her hands and knees with her back to Fleur. She was half-heartedly grumbling, 'Mr Buchanan's a lovely man, but such an untidy tyke at times!'

Taking the opportunity, Fleur scanned the writing. Yes, it was in the same arrogant tone as all the previous letters! Her heart hardened against the surgeon.

'Thank you, dear.' The housekeeper took the paper from Fleur and replaced it on the desk. 'If I didn't know he was a brilliant doctor, I'd really wonder about him. But he fixed our Davey's knee when he broke it at football, and now it's as good as new.' She sighed in admiration. 'Now, I'd do *anything* for Mr Buchanan.'

Suddenly the little woman cocked her ear. 'That sounds like Mr Buchanan's key in the front door . You stay here and I'll tell him you've come.'

She was gone before Fleur could make any

protest. And Fleur felt a little guilty about reading Max Buchanan's drafted letter. But, if she only kept her head and played cool, she might be able to prevent him from sending it. Clever tactics were called for, but she must use them.

In a matter of moments he strode into the study. It was a hot day, his shirt sleeves were rolled up over his elbows, and his collar and tie were loosened at his neck.

'This is a great surprise, Fleur.' He bent down and deposited his briefcase on a chair by the door. 'You'll stay for tea, of course.'

'I'd love that,' she replied as carefully as she could.

His open smile conveyed all his pleasure. Then over his shoulder he said, 'Yes, two for tea, Mrs Bramley. Let's have a nice selection of cakes, especially your almond slices.'

Sliding on to the leather chesterfield by her side, he spoke with a certain softness. 'It's great to see you.' Then more seriously, 'There isn't a problem with one of my patients, I hope?'

Fleur was glad of this opening to their conversation. She felt they were on neutral ground.

'No. . .no problem. Mrs Jolley is a delight to treat. She's totally co-operative, a perfect patient.'

'I presume her daughter isn't present, then!' His eyes sparkled mischievously.

Fleur had to smile back. 'No, she uses the time to go shopping.'

'Ah. . .' he murmured, 'that gives her mother a little peace and quiet, I should think.' He hesitated a moment. 'I wondered if I should have written a warning note on Mrs Jolley's notes—watch out, over-anxious daughter!'

'I'm sure she only wanted the best treatment,' Fleur defended. 'And however badly a person behaves on one occasion, I don't think it's fair to write it down and label them for life.'

Max Buchanan studied her face intently. 'No, a bad label can be just as disabling as a physical complaint.'

Fleur wondered at the slight harshness that had crept into his tone. Could he be thinking of something related to himself?

Mrs Bramley knocked before pushing in a stainless steel trolley laden with food and drink. After pouring the tea she left. Fleur thought she looked remarkably pleased about something.

'I think she's taken a shine to you, Fleur,' said Max Buchanan. 'Mrs Bramley only serves my most favoured guests with the best bone china. What were you talking about before I came home?'

A spurt of guilt made Fleur blush slightly, as she remembered reading the journal letter. Speaking a little flusteredly, she said, 'Nothing important, Mr Buchanan.' Then, rushing on, she remembered. 'Oh yes, she told me you'd fixed her Davey's knee. But I don't know who Davey is.'

'Her youngest son, her pride and joy. But you call me Max when you're in the house with me.'

'OK,' she replied softly. This man really had the most beautiful sooty black eyelashes. Then, recovering herself, 'I nearly forgot, I had to give Mrs Jolley a hot pack. She tended to fall asleep all the time, so short-wave might have been a dangerous treatment.'

'Well thought out,' he approved, as he sipped his tea.

'Actually, it was Miss Majors' idea. But we worked it out together.'

Then, remembering the very reason why she had come, she continued, 'Miss Majors has sent you an electrotherapy book.' She indicated that it was on his desk.

Without breaking his gaze he answered, 'I'll save that as my book at bedtime.' And the glint of wickedness in his eyes left her in no doubt that he could think of better things to do between his sheets.

He was mesmerising her. She must pull her mind back to reality. And the reality was the row in the medical journal that was so upsetting her father.

After staring into her teacup for a few moments she said, 'I don't think it'll be necessary for you to answer any more letters from my father in the *Journal*.'

'Why?' He widened his eyes slightly in surprise.

'My father is concentrating on a research proposal right now. He hopes to win one of the large grants from the University.'

'Hmm. . . Is this for a study into the position of the feet in standing?'

'Yes.' She tried to sound confident. 'He thinks it'll prove his theories.'

Max put down his cup and saucer. 'I wish your father luck with the grant. Heaven knows funds are scarce enough. But I hope he isn't going to bring as much bias into his research methods and design as he puts in his letters.'

Fleur felt her cheeks burn and her temper rise. 'Clear thinking is a first essential to good research and valid proof. And my father's work will do all that!'

To stem the rising tide in her voice, Max said, 'You seem to think that there's some personal dispute between your father and myself. I can assure you this isn't so. In medical science, particularly research, the whole thing is ongoing. There will always be corrections and amendments, whatever the results.'

'I should say that remark was certainly biased!' she bit back.

'It wasn't intended to be, Fleur.' There was a calmness in his voice. Then more firmly, 'Anyone can learn from another's mistakes——'

'How dare you criticise my father——!'

'If you'd only let me finish, Fleur, I would have said anyone can learn from another's mistakes as well as their successes. We shall have to judge from the results.'

Through narrowed blue eyes, she watched as he steadied his breathing.

'Ever since our quarrel in the car park I had the idea you might be a fiery young woman.' Now his eyes sparked as he caught and held her gaze. 'You're a real little fire-cat, Fleur. Did your mother wean you on tiger's milk?'

There was a hint of humour in his last sentence, but it was lost on Fleur. By bringing up the subject of her mother, Max had innocently touched on the cause of Professor Villiers' depression. Of course, he had no knowledge of these personal events.

This was too much for her. She wasn't thinking logically now. She automatically raised her hand to slap his face.

Catching her hand in mid-air, he exclaimed, 'Goodness, your temper can be physical too!

It's a good job my reflexes are sharp, otherwise you'd have scratched my face.'

Fleur's temper was rising second by second. And this arrogant man still held her hand captive. 'Tigers have claws, you know, Max. And sometimes we use them.'

'Aha, so you're a fighting she-cat too! I've heard tell that a fighting she-cat scratches her mate's face——'

She snatched her hand out of his grasp. She was feeling very wary.

Max continued provocatively slowly, 'But only in the mating season.'

Her face flushed crimson at this, and she stood up, trying to control herself. '*You* may look upon me as a she-cat weaned on tiger's milk, Mr Buchanan. But I suddenly feel very human!'

She made to escape towards the door, but he was after her immediately, and leaning his hand on it he effectively barred her exit.

'I'm delighted you're human, Fleur, and even more pleased that you're the female of the species.'

With a skilful gliding movement he turned her in his arms, holding her captive and close. Then he kissed her half-open surprised mouth with passion.

She tried to struggle and free her body. She tried to avert her face, but his lips were full of mastery, and she began to tremble and vibrate under his caresses. For a moment she felt she was melting against his hard muscular frame, and against all her logical will her eyes fluttered closed while the warmth and scent of this man wrought a magical spell.

She felt the individual touch of his kiss thrill her through and through. And when he delicately traced the line of her upper lip with his fingertip, his tenderness was transmitted to her and she quivered inside.

His voice was softly penetrating. 'Let's not argue, Fleur. Nothing I could ever write or say could harm your father's outstanding contribution to anatomy, or detract from his brilliant reputation.'

She looked into his eyes, so close to hers now, and they were keen and darkly dilated. But a semblance of logic surfaced through the haze in her dazzled brain.

Speaking breathlessly, she said, 'Please don't write any more letters to my father in the *Journal*. It upsets him so much.'

'But I've told you, Fleur, nothing can overturn your father's stature in the medical world.'

'Stop sending the letters,' she pleaded. A mist began to cover her dark blue eyes. She felt his breath fanning her cheek as he sighed.

'I can't do that. It would look as though I've backed down and can't fight on a scientific basis.'

He pulled her close again and was about to stroke her cheek when she broke away furiously and spat out,

'Fight! Yes, that's exactly what you want to do. You see my father as old and failing, and that's why you relentlessly pursue him. You just want to score academic points!'

'What nonsense——'

She wrenched her body free and ran out through the hall and the front door. There were tears streaming down her face as she heard Max repeatedly calling her name after her.

Halfway up the road and round a corner she was sobbing quietly and breathing heavily. And she had achieved nothing!

Even with all her planning Max had got the better of her tactics, and the better of her body. She recoiled inwardly in shame as she remembered how shamelessly she'd wanted and had kissed him. And to top it all, she hadn't prevented him from sending the letter. Losing her temper and losing her inhibitions had made her fail.

Was there any possible way to win against such a man?

CHAPTER FOUR

'I FEEL positively hopeful about this research proposal of mine.' That same evening Professor Villiers was sitting with Fleur in his study. And he confidently tapped the sheaf of notes that lay across his knees.

Fleur, who had been staring out of the window at the setting sun, replied, 'If hard work has got anything to do with it, the grant committee should give you the money straight away.'

'I know there's a good deal of competition from the younger fellows,' her father continued. 'But I think I've put down the objectives and the significance of my study very well.'

'Your review of the past literature was exhaustive, Dad. You've even gone back as far as Leonardo.'

The Professor nodded and continued to talk about his operational definitions.

Fleur's concentration wavered. Her mind drifted back to Max. She had used Leonardo to support her father, when she and Max had quarrelled in the car park. That had been a subdued argument compared to the passionate time in Max's study. And absently she drew her index finger across her upper lip.

Her father was talking of the practical considerations of his proposed study. He was going through the budget summary. Again, Fleur tuned her mind away. Cost-effectiveness was a fact of patient treatment at the hospital, even at student level.

In the evening half-light she studied her father's face. Although he looked bright about the proposed research and all the work, there was a weariness to his body.

There was a certain shortness of breath as he spoke now. Was it sheer exhaustion and worry? Or was he working himself into a real condition of ill-health?

The telephone in the hall jangled, and she stood up immediately. 'I'll get that, Dad.'

In the hallway she lifted the phone and said, 'Hello.' Then she gave the telephone number.

'Hello, is that you, Fleur?'

'Yes,' she replied automatically. She thought she should recognise this voice with its clear-cut tones. But she wasn't sure from where.

'This is Max. I've been terribly worried about you, Fleur. You were so distressed when you ran out of the house.'

Her heart began to pound within her chest. Why hadn't she recognised that distinctive voice? But she hadn't expected to speak to him here in her father's house.

The door to the study swung open and Professor Villiers popped his head round. 'Who's that? Anyone for me?'

If her father guessed who she was speaking to, and if he had any knowledge of what had happened with his arch-rival only hours ago, then he would surely have a heart attack on the spot.

In her confusion Fleur hurriedly placed her fingers over the mouthpiece so that Max could not hear. But in her agitation her fingers were spread apart, and the surgeon heard every word.

'It's not for you, Dad. It's Trev from the School.'

'Ah. . .that funny young man. Well, if you're going out tonight, darling, don't forget your front door key. I might work late on the proposal, and I don't want to be disturbed.'

When Professor Villiers shut the door to his study and retreated inside, Fleur sighed with relief. She had deceived him so far.

Removing her fingers from the mouthpiece, she took a deep breath and hissed, 'Why are you ringing me at home? Where did you get the number?'

'I got your father's number from the directory. And I'm ringing you because I'm very concerned.'

She could feel her chest begin to tighten. 'There's nothing for you to be concerned about. I'm perfectly all right. There's nothing more to say——'

'I think there is,' Max cut in swiftly. 'I think we should discuss this whole issue. Let me pick you up tonight, and we can go out to a restaurant, for a drive, anything you like.'

'I'm helping my father tonight.'

His sigh was protracted. 'No, you're not, Fleur. I know your father thinks you're going out with someone called Trev.'

'How did you hear that?' She could scarcely conceal the astonishment in her voice.

'Because, as clever and as charming as you are, Fleur, you'd never make a super sleuth or an undercover agent. I heard every word you said—obviously your hand wasn't completely clamped over the mouthpiece.'

She was furious with herself for being so careless. There was an uneasy silence, then Max said, 'Let me call round for you in, say. . .half an hour. I want to see you, if only to make sure you're all right.'

'I've told you, Max, there's nothing for *you* to bother about,' she half-whispered exasperatedly. She could hear her father moving about in the study, and he might come out again at any moment.

Then, far too formally, she ended the conversation. 'I don't think we have anything more to say to each other under the circumstances,' and she put the phone down hastily.

She ran headlong up the first flight of stairs and she shut herself in her bedroom. Her body trembled violently. It had been a shock to speak to Max again. And he had sounded so genuinely concerned about her. The whole problem was growing out of proportion. It seemed that everything revolved around Max, and she could think of nothing but him.

To clear her head she decided to do some study, and she pulled out, at random, a textbook from her shelf.

Sitting down at her little desk in front of the window, she gasped as she saw that she had chosen a textbook of electrotherapy. The very textbook that she had taken to Max, and he had said it would be his book at bedtime.

Abruptly she pushed it back on her shelf, and selected another on cardiology. But as she tried hard to concentrate, a cool, clear dawning focused in her mind.

Max had the power to instil desire in her heart. It was a condition that she was trying to fight. But, however hard she might search her textbook on cardiology, no remedy would be found.

Fleur was thankful that she hadn't come into contact with Max since the telephone conversation. But today was Friday, and there would be no getting out of it in a few hours' time. She wasn't looking forward to his evening lecture.

However, there would be one more problem for her this afternoon. She was to treat Pete Lowe.

All this week Ros had been seconded to the Barnes Centre where she would learn more about the treatment of cerebral palsied children. Pete had been laid low with the remains of a summer cold, but he had rung the department to say that he was fit for his treatment today.

With a bit of juggling, Fleur had managed to make time for him. He was to be her last patient of the day.

When she emerged from a treatment cubicle, where she had settled Mrs Jolley with her hot pack, she saw Pete in a wheelchair. He was being pushed by one of the ambulancemen.

'Hello, Pete,' she greeted. Then to the ambulance man, 'Could we go into this cubicle, please, because if has the special hydraulic plinth.'

'Certainly,' the man replied. 'Here we go, squire.'

As they helped Pete to transfer on to the plinth he gave a stream of continual muttered instructions.

'Let the ambulanceman do this, Miss Villiers. He's more used to transfers.'

Fleur took no offence and stood back. 'Of course,' she agreed. 'You two know the best way by now.'

It was a good job that Pete was already dressed in his shorts, because the whole procedure was taking a very long time.

'I've got pain everywhere today,' he rasped as he sat on the plinth.

'You look as though you haven't been sleeping well,' Fleur commented.

'Got it in one!'

It took even more time for the ambulanceman and Fleur to position Pete comfortably in the lying position with his legs in elevation. This was so he could have the Jobst intermittent pressure treatment.

Finally they thanked the ambulanceman and he left. Then Pete shook his head wearily. 'I certainly need some of that restorative sleep that Miss Majors spoke about. I'm knackered as soon as I get into bed. I wouldn't mind if I was knackered by the middle of the night. It's so unfair on my wife.'

Fleur, who was bending down with her back to Pete so that she could plug in the Jobst, opened her eyes wide. Here was a candid admission. And she flushed a little.

By now she was quite used to patients asking questions about intimate problems. But she had never been asked about anything sexual.

Before she had time to collect her embarrassed thoughts, Pete spoke again. 'I only made the effort to come to Physio today because I knew you'd be treating me. Mrs Lindy says you know what you're doing. And everyone calls you "the anatomy physio".'

Fleur laughed at the reminder of her nickname, and she felt relieved that Pete had so quickly sidestepped the issue of his sex life.

Pete continued to give exact directions about how to roll on his Tubigauze, and then his Jobst boot. Because Fleur hadn't had that much practice with this particular machine and it took some time to connect the air hose, and make sure that the pressures were exactly right, she found she was running way behind schedule.

Finally she managed to check Mrs Jolley, but she was perfectly happy and had just four minutes left on her hot pack.

So Fleur settled herself at the students' desk. She wished Ros were here to treat Pete. She was sure that he was obliquely asking for some sexual counselling. But Fleur didn't feel competent enough to give this. Basically she was embarrassed, so she made a note on Pete's file.

Lectures on sexual psychology had been arranged for the final-year students. But that wasn't for a month or so. Although Fleur had gone out with many men over the years, she had never liked any of them enough to sleep with one.

Mrs Jolley's pinger rang out, letting Fleur know that the hot pack time was up. Returning to the cubicle, Fleur removed the heat treatment and checked the skin.

'That looks fine,' she commented. There were no signs of burns.

'That moist heat is so relaxing.' Mrs Jolley spoke slowly as if in a dream. 'My mind wanders back to the old days when I'm lying like this.' A soft smile spread over her face.

Fleur sat with her patient as the elderly lady went through her exercise routine. Mrs Jolley remembered everything perfectly, even the fact that she wasn't to force the flexion because of her osteophytes.

Then Fleur demonstrated the correct way to pick up a heavy object. 'Always use your knees to get the thrust for the lift. Never lift anything with a bent or a twisted back.'

She then made Mrs Jolley go through the procedure by lifting an empty cardboard box. 'Well, you've mastered that technique too,' she commended.

However, as the elderly lady was preparing to leave she accidentally dropped her straw hat, and she bent to retrieve it, using a curved spine.

'Now, that was a classic mistake,' Fleur rebuffed gently. 'You lifted the box correctly, but not your lightweight hat.'

'But I thought the lifting techniques were only for heavy things.'

'No, they're for all objects, whether they're as light as a feather or as heavy as a barrel of beer.'

Mrs Jolley didn't look convinced, so Fleur gave some more explanation. 'We frequently find that patients who've been doing heavy digging in their gardens have no problem while doing the digging. But say an hour later, when they bend to pick up a single leaf from the lawn, then they'll feel a sharp pain and they'll have damaged their disc.'

Raising her eyebrows, Mrs Jolley remarked, 'I'll have to tell my son-in-law that. The other evening he jumped up out of his easy chair, rushed out of the sitting-room and picked up a blackbird's feather that had fluttered on to the lawn.'

Fleur was surprised to see her patient's normally immobile face crease into a smile, and something like a saucy glint lit her eyes.

After she had safely delivered Mrs Jolley to her daughter, it was time to go back to Pete. The massage technique for removing the œdematous swelling at his ankle proved to be harder work than she had imagined.

It was physically hard to execute the massage strokes effectively, and she had to be very careful, because Pete frequently gave loud instructions about sore spots.

Fleur inspected his foot carefully. 'Have you strained it lately, Pete?' she asked.

'No,' he replied wearily. 'It's just that "fibrositis" sort of pain that springs up anywhere. It's that thing that Miss Majors was talking about. It comes when I haven't had my restorative sleep.'

By ten minutes to five Fleur had only just finished the massage, and she hadn't even started on the passive or active movements. She could hear the ambulanceman enquiring about Pete.

'Can we give the rest of the treatment a miss today?' Pete asked. 'I can do my exercises at home, and I don't want to keep everyone in the ambulance waiting.'

He looked so tired that Fleur agreed. And there was another factor looming in her mind. Max's lecture was about to start at any moment, and she was going to be late.

Helping Pete to put on his shoes and socks, and standing by as he was transferred into his wheelchair, took up more time.

So by the time Fleur was racing up the stairs in the School of Physiotherapy, the hall clock read five-fifteen. And at the top flight she stood motionless.

Ahead of her lay a large landing and to her

right the classroom where Max was lecturing. She could hear his muffled tones because this classroom had windows that looked out on to the landing.

Cautiously she leaned forward and glanced through the nearest window. Max was turning to write on the board. She drew back instantly. Luckily he hadn't seen her.

Fleur did not fancy a confrontation with the consultant. If she walked in late she was sure he would only make some sarcastic comment that would amuse the class.

Ahead of the classroom lay the girls' locker-room. If she could sneak by without being noticed, she could miss him altogether.

She surveyed the two windows on the side of the class. They reached from ceiling to desk height. Now if she could crawl along the floor under the windows then no one would suspect her presence.

The landing was completely deserted, so she determined to do just this. And as she hitched up her white dress and began crawling along she hugged the wall, and something like a physical thrill vibrated all her nerve-endings,

Slowly and carefully she manoeuvred her way past the first window. Very soon she was under the second window and almost before the door.

In her excitement she was breathing more

rapidly now, and she cocked her ear to listen. Her father's rival's voice was more distinct nearer the door.

The flow of his lecture sounded continuous. It appeared as if he was fully absorbed in his work.

Gingerly she lifted one hand to place it before the door, when a shaft of light, bright and halting, made her freeze. The door swung open, illuminating the area.

Then a charming voice, fully audible to the class, rang out. 'I see you don't want to be late for my lecture, Miss Villiers.'

Fleur was nearly dying of shame. She didn't want to look up.

Max bent down agilely and whispered close to her face, 'Really, Fleur, how can you stoop so low?'

She didn't know whether to laugh or burst into tears. But she stood up suddenly and muttered back, 'I've been with a patient, that's the only reason I'm late.'

He looked hugely amused by the whole affair. This made her blood begin to boil.

'Ah,' he replied in a laconic lilt, 'patients are always a good excuse.'

At this point Fleur lost her temper. She didn't know how she kept her voice subdued when she bit out, 'Go to the devil, Max!'

But with a nifty side-step he turned, and

ushered her into the classroom with the fully audible words, 'After you, Miss Villiers!'

Fleur was forced to enter the room first. And, being fully visible to the whole class, she could hardly answer back. It was almost impossible to keep a straight face while she walked to the back of the class and took up her seat at her desk.

To her fury, Max continued his talk as if nothing had happened. Only the slightest glint in his eyes betrayed the fact that he had been the winner.

Fleur hid her eyes behind her curved hand as she took notes. No one was cooler or more cutting than this surgeon. What an adversary! And he seemed to possess powers beyond all human capacity. He definitely had X-ray eyes!

After the lecture Fleur had supper with Ros. Her husband was out playing tennis.

Ros had shaken her head and thrown up her hands in despair at hearing the continuing Villiers/Buchanan saga.

But their conversation took a more serious turn when Fleur explained about Pete's problem. It was decided that Ros would organise some sexual counselling if Pete wanted this.

It was eight-fifteen that evening when Fleur turned the key in her front door lock. The house was quiet and very still. She presumed her father was still at the Faculty Club on the University.

But when she went into the kitchen to make herself a cup of coffee, she found her father sitting at the table with his head in his hands.

'What's the matter, Dad?' she asked.

His half-eaten supper had been pushed haphazardly to one side, and his eyes were surprised and absently blinking as he looked up.

'Oh, it's you, darling.'

Fleur grabbed a chair and sat on the opposite side of the table, and leant forward.

'Ach,' he began, and looked steadfastly at his hands, 'the Dean gave me a pretty piece of advice this afternoon. It seems that submitting my research proposal would be a complete waste of time.'

'Why?'

'Already the grant has been more or less allocated. It's a toss-up between two of the younger professors.'

Fleur felt her heart plummet. Her father withdrew a pocket handkerchief and blew his nose noisily.

'All that work wasted,' he continued bleakly.

'No, it can't be wasted!' she shot back, hoping to infuse her father with energy. 'What about a grant from the private sector? What about money from one of the big industrial companies?'

A glimmer of hope began to appear in the Professor's eyes. 'Of course! I'd forgotten that source.'

After a moment's silence when Fleur watched her father gearing himself up, he announced, 'I'm going back to the Faculty Club right now. Your father might be old, but he's not down and out yet.'

'That's the spirit, Dad!' Fleur came round the table and gave him a hug.

She followed him to the front door, but as his hand reached for the handle he hesitated. There was a faltering look in his eyes.

'They say setbacks come in batches,' he mumbled. 'And I suppose my next will be a damning letter in the *Journal* from that Buchanan!'

Fleur wished her father 'good luck' and watched him drive away. And just like her father, her resolve was up. The farce with Max outside the classroom only served to fuel her determination.

'He's not going to send another letter!' she ground out.

Fleur didn't know how she would prevent the letter from being published. All she knew was this. . .she had to win! And she would stand up and fight like a man!

CHAPTER FIVE

MAX himself opened the door. Fleur had given three sharp summonses on his brass knocker. He looked amazingly pleased to see her, and the fun sparkling in his brown eyes only annoyed her more.

'Hello, Fleur. How can I help you?' He stood back immediately to let her come in.

She strode purposefully into the front hall. 'I want a very serious talk with you,' she announced.

'Then we'll go into the study.' He raised his eyebrows slightly at her assertiveness, and stroked the dark stubble on his chin as he followed her. A serious concern clouded his eyes.

He indicated the chesterfield. 'Please sit down, Fleur.'

'I'd rather stand,' came the curt reply.

'Then I'll sit down.' He deliberately kept his voice subdued. Sitting down, he crossed one long leg over the other, and clasped his hands over his upper knee.

'Fire away, Fleur.'

'You've got to *stop* arguing with my father in the medical journal,' she blurted out. She could feel her whole body quivering with pent-up anger.

Clasping his interlaced fingers tighter, he remarked. 'You certainly know how to bark out your orders like a sergeant-major! Your father is capable and strong enough to defend himself. I can't imagine what's behind your attitude.'

It was too much—all too much. Her iron-willed resolve melted like wax, and she burst into tears.

She poured out the whole wretched past history—her mother's death, her father's inability to cope with his upcoming retirement, and now the stunning news that his research proposal had been rejected.

'So you see,' she sobbed, 'you've got to stop sending those letters. Otherwise I don't know what will happen. My father may well work himself into a heart attack.'

Immediately following this emotional outburst, Fleur felt a fool. She could hardly focus on Max because her eyes were running with tears. Hastily she wiped them away.

Silent seconds ticked away. She felt she would burst if he didn't say something.

Then slowly he rose and walked towards his desk. 'Look at this, Fleur.' He held a white envelope out towards her. His command was direct but soft.

'What is it?' she queried.

'It's my next letter to the medical journal. As you can see, it's sealed inside this addressed envelope.'

She clenched her teeth together. For two pins she could have snatched it from his hand and torn it to pieces in front of him.

He continued softly, 'You told me not to send the letter the last time you were here. And I've debated the matter many times.'

Fleur stared at the object. The address was typed, but there was no stamp on the envelope.

Suddenly he let it fall from his hand, and it landed face up in the waste paper basket next to his desk.

'I don't want to upset you, Fleur. Neither do I harbour any ill intentions towards your father. He's a man with a tremendous brain, and I've admired his work for years. As far as I'm concerned, the argument rests here.' He nudged the waste paper basket with his foot.

This was not the hard victory she had expected. And she suddenly felt very weak at the knees. It had been so easy and quick!

'Could I sit down?' she asked in a shaky voice.

'Of course—would you like a drink? A brandy or something? You look a bit shocked.'

'An orange juice would be lovely.'

'I'll get it from the fridge in the kitchen. It'll be ice-cold.'

When he re-entered the study, Max placed

a cut glass tumbler on the low table before the chesterfield. The he poured some drink from a bottle.

Gratefully she sipped it as he sat down beside her. Her composure was only slowly coming back.

'I want you to know one thing, though, Fleur,' he began as her breathing became calmer. 'Stopping these public letters is a hard thing for me to do. It will look as though I've admitted defeat.'

She held her breath.

'I've had a rough ride in the science world, ever since I entered medical school. It's because I studied music and composition at the Royal Academy.'

She turned her head to look at him. His eyes were gentle, but there was some pain there too.

'Doctors and other scientists look on my work suspiciously. They feel that my work stems from the arts, and that my roots must be bound to the emotions.' He raised his dark eyebrows. 'They feel I can't think logically and rationally.'

'That's a stupid way of thinking,' she protested. But she bit her lower lip as she remembered that her father had given that very same argument. 'Even Leonardo was a great genius in both the arts and the sciences.'

Max chuckled lightly. 'I'm hardly in the same

league as Leonardo, but the reminder of such a great man certainly gives me a boost, Fleur.'

She looked steadfastly into his face. 'I think I've been guilty of judging you on an emotional basis. When I watched how your letters affected my father, I thought you were a malicious man, who was spurred by vaulting ambition.'

He raised one dark eyebrow, but she hurried on.

'Now that I know a little more about you, I can understand your motives. And I believe that it's the act of a big man, to stop the letters.'

He nodded silently and a slow warmth lit his eyes.

'But I'm not at all sure that I understand you completely, Mr Buchanan. And I know to my cost that you have supra-normal powers.' She was laughing. 'I can only imagine you caught me creeping by your class this evening because you've got X-ray eyes!'

'Oh. Fleur, you're priceless!' he grinned. 'X-ray eyes are a fabulous idea. Imagine just how much easier and cheaper my work with patients would be. I wouldn't have to bother to send anyone to the Radiology Department.'

Her blue eyes sparkled back. 'No, seriously,' she continued, 'how did you catch me out this evening?'

'Quite easily. And I only had to use my normal twenty-twenty vision. I saw you peep-ing through that window that looks out on to the landing and then you bent down towards the floor. I knew you were about to crawl past the door and give me the slip when I saw a fleeting shadow.'

The merriment in her face shone out as she said, 'I could have kicked you for those clever one-liners.'

'Ah, about stooping too low, and ushering you to the devil in front of me. They were fun.'

'Yes,' she replied, playfully punching his shoulder.

But he caught her hand in mid-air and swiftly kissed her fingertips. 'Don't change for me.' he whispered. 'I like you just the way you are.'

His brilliant brown eyes were tense, and they began to dilate darkly. Fleur felt his powerful masculine mesmerism.

And when he took her face gently between his two large hands he kissed her tenderly at first. Something about Max made her melt inside. And she parted her lips naturally to receive his delicate probing tongue.

After some deeply passionate kisses when she stroked the shaved hair at the nape of his neck, she felt her body become fluid and molten with desire.

'Sweetheart, let's get more comfortable,' he said huskily, as he brushed her long fair hair behind her ear and nuzzled closer.

'Mmm. . .yes.'

He lifted her legs so that she was lying on the chesterfield. Then he slid up to her, the full length of his body against hers. As he continued to caress her back and slide his hand ever lower over her bottom, she felt shivers of pure sensation thrilling through her body.

His lovemaking was controlled and ever aware of her responses. She could feel the quiver and desire of his pulsing manhood. He was burning through the light fabric of her clothes against her stomach.

Taking her free hand in his, he pulled it down between their bodies, and she was completely caught up in the exquisite feel of him.

An antique wooden clock on his mantelpiece whirred and clicked noisily, then started chiming out the late hour.

Fleur tore her lips away from his and asked, 'What's the time? It's completely dark outside.'

'Only ten o'clock, sweetheart.' Then gruffly over his shoulder he threw an insult towards the offending timepiece. 'I shall muffle you with a Jones bandage in future!'

Rational common sense thinking began to infuse itself into Fleur's sensually drugged brain. Making love with Max was more thrilling and more exciting than she had ever dreamt possible.

Breathlessly she continued, 'I should be home when my father comes back from the Faculty Club.'

Tentatively she looked into his face. She thought he would be angry, but he pushed her tangled hair away from her forehead and spoke as with a great effort.

'It's one hell of a wrench to let you go, Fleur. Perhaps your father needs your company more than I do tonight. . .but let's have a few minutes more to ourselves. . .at least to cool down.'

So she lay nestled close to his chest, and felt his strong arms encircle her. And she felt that her love for him would grow more and more.

Reluctantly they parted that evening. Max walked her home, and kissed her goodbye softly in the shadows of the oak trees that lined the road.

'I've got to lecture in Leeds tomorrow.' He sounded dejected. 'I won't be back until the course finishes on Tuesday.'

'Oh, no!' she sighed in a small voice.

But they agreed to meet again on Tuesday evening.

Her father was buoyed up again when she spoke to him in the lounge. He had found out from a faculty member that there was a big research grant available from the chemical giant HDH, and he was determined to enter for it.

It was also fortunate that her father presumed that she had spent the evening with Trev. Fleur didn't enlighten him. He would soon come round to thinking that Max was a good and honourable man, especially now there were to be no more letters.

So she was enormously pleased that night as she slipped between the sheets. Thoughts of Max made her deliciously happy, and she fell asleep thinking of his super husky voice.

Fleur stood close to Ros in the only quiet place in the Physiotherapy Department. . .the weight-lifting area in the big gym. It was Tuesday afternoon.

'I'm glad things have been sorted out for Pete,' said Fleur.

'It's taken quite a bit of organisation,' explained Ros. 'I got a lot of help from Miss Majors too.'

'Hmm. . .' Fleur bit her lip. 'So Pete's rheumatologist thinks he could be heading for a flare-up with his disease?'

'It's unfortunate, but that's the way things look at the moment. The problem with sleep might be an indication of this. Anyway, I've made an appointment for Pete to see the consultant later this week.'

'And after that, Pete will see the medical

social worker with special training in sexual counselling?'

Ros continued, 'Yes, that's right. If Pete and his wife are the sort of couple who can communicate well with each other, then the sexual problem shouldn't be too difficult.'

'I noticed that you took him into the clinical instructor's room for a chat,' remarked Fleur.

'Yes. Miss Majors said that something like this was too delicate a matter, and could easily be overheard in the main Physio area.' Ros looked very satisfied as she said,' And you know, Pete was so pleased, he almost jumped out of his wheelchair when I'd organised his appointments and the ambulance.'

Suddenly they heard a buzz and a mounting commotion coming from the front reception. They hurried out to the area, only to see Miss Majors ushering Mrs Highbrown-Clack and Mrs Jolley into her office.

'What on earth's all that about?' asked Fleur.

'Goodness knows! But something's up.'

Ros was disappointed that she had to dash away to treat a patient. But it was approaching Mrs Jolley's treatment time, so Fleur walked restlessly up and down outside the office.

She could hear the clinical instructress trying to make soothing noises. But these were frequently interrupted by gabbled high-pitched exclamations from Mrs Highbrown-

Clack, Fleur couldn't hear a peep from Mrs Jolley. She began to feel anxious.

Shortly Miss Majors appeared and shut the door behind her. 'Ah, Miss Villiers, I'm glad to find you.'

'Is Mrs Jolley all right?' asked Fleur.

Miss Majors' normally controlled features took on an addled look. 'It seems that Mrs Jolley has been the victim of a granny hijack,' she explained.

Fleur's mouth dropped open in surprise.

'But for goodness' sake don't mention that phrase "granny hijack" in front of the daughter—it'll only set her off again. I can't get any sense out of the woman, she keeps returning to the price of the new car that's been stolen.'

Even after this explanation, Fleur didn't feel at all enlightened.

'I think both mother and daughter ought to see a doctor,' Miss Majors continued.

'Mr Buchanan is taking a clinic next door,' Fleur supplied eagerly.

'Excellent! Pop along and see if he can fit them in.'

Fleur explained the situation to the physio in charge of the clinic. Luckily Max was on his own at the moment.

Fleur knocked loudly and walked in. Max's pensive face creased into an open grin as he saw her. He had been reading X-rays at a viewer.

'What are you doing here?' He strode forward and kissed her lightly.

The explanation of the abduction put him immediately on his professional alert. 'Send them into the examination cubicle next door. I'll see them straight away.'

Both Fleur and Max helped Mrs Jolley on to the plinth. Then Fleur pulled out a chair for Mrs Highbrown-Clack, who was turning more puce by the minute.

'Were you hurt at all, Mrs Jolley?' Max enquired gently.

'Oh, no, dear. The two young men were very polite.'

Half sitting on the plinth nearer to his patient, Max continued, 'Now, tell me exactly what happened.'

Mrs Highbrown-Clack interrupted. 'I was in the bank withdrawing some shopping money. I'd left my mother in the car outside. When I came out the car had gone!'

'Please calm yourself,' Max advised. 'But what exactly happened to *you*, Mrs Jolley?'

'Well, I was sitting in the back seat; then suddenly two young men got in, and off we went.'

Surprisingly, Mrs Jolley didn't look at all put out. From the gleam in her eye she had viewed the episode as a grand escapade.

'Did they deliberately abduct the car with you in it?'

'Oh, I don't think so. We were driving along, rather too fast, I think, so I tapped the one on the shoulder. He had a bit of a start. . .but he was quite a good driver. We only mounted the pavement once.'

Mrs Highbrown-Clack groaned and slumped on her chair.

'And then what happened?' encouraged Max.

'Well, I told the two boys that I should be in treatment having my physio so they very kindly helped me out of the car, sat me on a low wall and phoned the bank to let my daughter know where I was.'

Is this story for real? thought Fleur.

Mrs Highbrown-Clack started up again. 'Yes, I had to get a taxi, and pick my mother up. The bank phoned the police. But I haven't had the courage to let Mr Highbrown-Clack know. I don't know what he'll say. That new-registration four-door white Mercedes was his baby.'

Max cut in, 'Then I suggest you ring your husband right away. There's a pay-phone in the corridor outside.' With this advice she scurried out.

And in the more peaceful atmosphere Max gave Mrs Jolley a thorough examination. When he'd taken her blood pressure he raised his eyebrows and said, 'You appear to have taken all this in your stride. But I think it would be a good idea if you rested now. Shock has a habit of catching up.'

'But while I'm here can't I have my physio?'

Max looked a little dumbfounded, then replied, 'Yes. Miss Villiers can give you your hot pack, as long as she stays with you to keep an eye on you. But leave your exercises for today.'

As ordered, Fleur sat with Mrs Jolley while she had her superficial heat treatment. 'Your daughter has phoned the police,' Fleur explained. 'A policeman will come to interview you. What he'll really need is a good description of the two lads who took the car. Can you remember them?'

'Oh, yes,' Mrs Jolley beamed. 'They were both tall, dark and handsome.'

Fleur didn't think this would be of much help. 'And what were they wearing?' she asked.

'Ah, now I remember that. Tight jeans, and short-sleeved T-shirts that showed the muscles of their shoulders.' A gleam came into her eyes as she recalled this.

Fleur tried not to smile. If this was all the description the police would get, she didn't think the lads would be caught.

Mrs Jolley went on, a serene smile on her face, 'You know, today has reminded me of a lot of good things in my life. Today I feel like a young girl in my heart.' She sighed. 'You see, when my fellow Tom and I were courting, we had a very hard time of it. I was only a cook in a barrister's house, and Tom's family ran a garage. They thought I was beneath their Tom.'

She compressed her lips, then went on, 'But love will find a way. One night Tom took the fanciest car from the garage showroom—a vintage Rolls-Royce—and we flew to Gretna Green and got married.' She laughed with delight at the memories.

'It sounds very romantic,' said Fleur.

'Yes, dear, I had a wonderful marriage. My man was a spunky fella.' She gave Fleur a significant look. 'I hope you've got a nice young man, Miss Villiers.'

Fleur thought of Max, and answered with a smile, 'Yes, you certainly could call him a spunky fella.'

By the end of her treatment Mrs Jolley still showed no signs of going into shock, so Fleur escorted her into the waiting area. She left her sitting near the open door, sitting next to her daughter.

A few minutes later a middle-aged policeman arrived. He spoke very seriously to Fleur. 'I believe you're treating a Mrs Jolley, a poor old lady who's been involved in a madcap abduction.'

'Yes, Mrs Jolley's in the waiting area. I'll take you along.' Fleur pointed out her patient.

'There she is. She's wearing her straw hat with panache.'

The policeman's solemn face took on a look of shocked amazement. Surrounding the 'poor old lady' was a circle of listeners. Some stood, some sat in wheelchairs, and all were eagerly listening to the grand account of today's great adventure.

Fleur added, 'If you'd like some privacy for your interview, I'm sure you could use our clinical instructor's office.' She indicated the room.

'Thanks, miss,' came the stunned reply. 'I think that might be very necessary.'

As Fleur left the scene, she saw Mrs Jolley in high spirits. And sitting to one side, a solitary figure, Mrs Highbrown-Clack. Her designer clothes looked positively ruffled. The revers of her tailored suit were set askew. Her skirt was half hitched up, and her legs stuck out in front at an angle that at best could not be described as ladylike.

Sometimes there were odd turn-arounds in life. Mrs Jolley looked rejuvenated. And this wasn't the effect of modern medicine, or any treatment available in the Physiotherapy Department, but the revival of memories of a spunky fella.

When Fleur came home that evening from the physio school, she found a recorded message from her father on the answerphone. He would have supper at the Faculty Club, and he wasn't sure what time he'd be home.

One of the new and aspiring statisticians at the University had agreed to help him with the statistics in his research design. Fleur was delighted to hear the enthusiasm in her father's voice. And it lessened some of the guilt she felt about seeing Max behind her father's back.

After a light meal, she showered and took time to brush a shine into her long hair. Then she chose a cool cotton dress that complemented the transparent blue of her eyes. And she headed excitedly for Dolphin Road.

As she turned into the entrance of number sixty-two, she was totally unaware of a familiar car, and a familiar face on the opposite side of the crossroads. Her father's puzzled concern was completely concealed from her.

She was about to reach for the brass knocker when the door swung open silently. Fleur was confronted with a pair of smiling grey eyes. Here was a woman she had never seen before.

CHAPTER SIX

'HELLO, deary. You must be Miss Fleur.' The older woman saw Fleur's surprise, and added, 'I'm Mrs Pippin. Mrs Bramley's on holiday. Pleased to meet you.'

'I'm pleased to meet you too.' Fleur held out her hand.

Mrs Pippin quickly transferred her brass-cleaning materials to a hall table, and shook hands warmly.

'Mr Buchanan's expecting you. He's playing his music in the lounge at the moment.'

Fleur walked into the hall, and was greeted by the big romantic sound of a Steinway piano. Although the door to the lounge was shut, Max's music permeated the whole house.

The housekeeper cautioned Fleur with a half-raised hand. 'Do listen to this music. He's been playing it over and over this evening, and I love it.'

Like Mrs Pippin, Fleur stood spellbound by the sound. The music had charm and power. There were exquisite moments of phrasing, and as the piece progressed she felt the passion and artistry in the work.

The surgeon's music grew in poetry and

power until it ended exultantly.

'He's ready for you now, miss,' Mrs Pippin whispered.

She opened the door and pushed Fleur gently into the room. As the fading sound of the music reverberated around the walls, Fleur felt her senses resonate.

Max was sitting with his head bowed. Fleur dared not speak, she dared not break the spell. It seemed as if it was so precious and intimate.

But he sensed her presence and swivelled round on his piano stool. 'I didn't know you were here, sweetheart.'

The warmth in his eyes sparkled. It touched something deep inside her, and she was caught and held quite willingly.

He stood up and held both his hands slowly out to her. Instantly she ran into his arms, and there returned his passionate kisses.

Breathlessly she drew away from his face. 'That music was beautiful. I've never heard it before. What's it called?'

'Whatever you like. I was thinking of you when I composed it.'

A thrill leapt through her veins. Her hands reached up to stroke the nape of his neck, and she kissed Max more passionately than she had ever kissed anyone in her life.

With his free hand he reached down and played a trill on the high notes of the piano.

Laughingly she broke free of his lips and

cried, 'You're wonderfully crazy! You do the most unexpected things.'

'Of course,' he replied with a grin. 'You almost took my breath away with that last kiss. I could hardly speak at the same time, so I had to let you know how I felt somehow. So it was through my music.'

She laughed again and slid her hands around his waist, hugging him close to her. After a few moments she felt a restraining tension spread through his body. And when she looked up into his face, she saw a serious, almost pained expression.

He spoke softly. 'I had many things planned for tonight, Fleur; but they'll all have to be shelved for a few weeks.'

'Why, what's happened?'

Taking her hand, he led her to a low moss-green sofa. He sat close to her with one arm around her shoulder and the other around her waist.

'Months ago I arranged a sabbatical with several of the leading hospitals on the west coast of North America. I should have been flying out early tomorrow morning, but some foul-up with the airlines means that I must go tonight.'

'Oh, no. . .' she replied in a small choked voice. 'How long have we got together?'

Max checked his watch. 'Less than forty minutes.' He sounded equally deflated.

'And how long will you be away?'

'Thirty-two days, to be exact,' he groaned. Then looking steadfastly into her eyes, 'Not being able to see and feel and hold you close will make me feel a wreck.'

'I'm aching now at the thought of such a separation,' Fleur said desperately.

Max tipped her chin up so that he could look into her downcast eyes. 'I want to make love to you, Fleur. I want to fully satisfy you. But I want our first time to be memorable, and not a hurried rush.'

Fleur was shocked at his bluntness. But, no doubt about it, her body clamoured for him just as much.

They spoke intimately to one another, revealing their innermost feelings. And Fleur told Max Mrs Jolley's story about the spunky fella.

Max was hugely amused, and when he laughed she felt his powerful torso vibrate close to hers.

Then he said, '*This* spunky fella will be devastated without you, Fleur. And damn the time, it's almost ready for me to go. Give me your phone number so I can ring while I'm away.'

She had been caught up with the magic of the moment, but reality sent a shiver down her spine. 'Don't phone.' She turned her head away. 'I don't want my father to know about us. Not just yet.' She heard his sigh.

'Then I suppose you don't want me to write either?'

She turned back quickly. 'I would love your letters, but. . .'

'But your father would ask questions.'

She nodded silently.

'Then I'll just have to be your secret champion of romance, Fleur. But always remember this. I shall be thinking of you; when I shave in the morning, when I give lectures, and when I'm at all the social events.'

They said their goodbyes, and Fleur left him with a parting kiss and said, 'Take care, Max. God speed you back to me.'

'Who were you visiting earlier this evening in Dolphin Road, Fleur?'

Her father's question took her completely off guard. She opened a kitchen cupboard and hid her face behind the door as she pretended to look for the jar of coffee.

She needed a few moments to collect her thoughts, because she had never been able to lie to her father. And she knew by the tone in his question that he already knew the answer. So she decided to transpose time and events.

'Miss Majors asked me to deliver an electrotherapy textbook to Mr Buchanan. Apparently he wanted to read up on the subject.'

She tried to sound as casual as possible. After she had arranged the coffee mugs on the sideboard, she turned and caught the cold look in her father's eye.

'Why must Miss Majors use you as a courier?'

Fleur already had that answer. 'She had to supervise the cerebral palsied children for their swimming lessons this evening. Otherwise she would have taken it herself.'

The electric kettle began to whistle, so she busied herself preparing the hot drinks. When at last she sat with her father at the kichen table, he continued, 'Be careful of Buchanan. I've heard that he's as handsome as the devil, and you. . .you're more beautiful than your mother, if that's possible.'

Fleur felt sad to hear this. But she had to remain on her guard.

'Don't be dazzled by Buchanan,' the professor went on. 'He's cunning and clever, and may well use you to find out information about my research.'

'Don't be ridiculous, Dad!' she shot back, a little too forcefully. Then with a little more control she shrugged. 'He was playing his piano this evening. I hardly saw him.'

'Ah. . ."the music doctor",' he retorted derisively. 'Well, as long as the man only plays tra-la-la on his instrument, and not oh-la-la on my daughter!'

Fleur was shocked at the hostility in her father's tone. And it caused her much emotional conflict in her heart. The short time with Max this evening had been almost idyllic. She was still stunned by the music he had composed for her; and his comedy act when he had played the light trill on the piano during their kiss still made her smile.

She spooned sugar into her coffee mug. 'I don't think he'll be a problem to you, Dad. He's off on some American tour. He'll be so busy, I doubt you'll get another letter in the *Journal*.'

'That's twice you've told me not to expect a reply in the *Journal*,' he replied evenly. 'Let's hope your prophecy turns out to be correct.'

Because Fleur believed so ardently in Max, she easily put her father's negative feelings to one side. And as she counted down the days to her lover's return, she missed him more and more.

'Heavens to Betsy! That last class with Miss Majors wasn't exactly the bee's knees,' mimicked Trevor.

He and Fleur sat in the students' area of the main Physio Department while their patients were undergoing heat treatments.

'You keep your voice down,' Fleur urged. 'Miss Majors is somewhere around, and you know she has the habit of getting the better of your smart remarks.'

'Huh. . .' he conceded grudgingly. 'She's on the case most of the time, but this abdominal massage for constipation must originate from the days of the medieval knights.'

Fleur shook her head, but privately she had to agree.

'How about laying a wager with me?' Trevor continued. 'I'll eat my *Gray's Anatomy* textbook if anyone in our class gives an abdominal massage for constipation at any time during their career.'

'No bet, because I agree with you,' she giggled.

Just then Miss Majors appeared from nowhere. This gave Trevor a visible start.

'Have either of you two students done your stint at the Barnes Centre with the CP children?' Miss Majors enquired.

'No,' they replied in unison.

'A cerebral palsied child has turned up for treatment today, but her qualified physio is off sick.' She contemplated the two of them openly, then after raising an eyebrow at Trevor said, 'I must have somebody sensible to treat the child. Miss Villiers, you can volunteer.'

Fleur gulped.

Miss Majors continued, 'The child's name is Wendy Hitchins. She's here with her father.

They can wait until you have free time, their appointment isn't for another ten minutes.'

Fleur had to forcibly restrain her vocal cords. She almost answered back, 'Yes, Miss Sergeant-Majors.'

It was a tight squeeze to finish off the treatment of her present patient in time. But she did it. Then she walked into the reception area and looked about for the little girl and her father.

She saw the only likely-looking duo sitting at the far end, well away from the other patients. The father was in his late thirties. He was thin, and there was a worried, almost exasperated expression on his face.

The little girl was about eight years old. She was well cared for, and her hair had been brushed into ringlets. But she was restless as her father tried to hold her on his knee.

Fleur introduced herself and explained the situation.

Mr Hitchins said thank you several times, then, 'I don't know if Wendy is going to be very co-operative for her treatment today. I'm afraid she's a bit cranky.'

Fleur pushed her fingers into the little girl's hand. But she pulled her floppy arm away immediately, and made a grizzling sound. She rolled her head on her father's chest, and Fleur could see that the treatment wasn't going to be an easy one.

'Excuse me a few moments, Mr Hitchins, but I have to find Wendy's treatment card,' she said.

She left and walked briskly into the qualified section of the department. Here she was immediately confronted with a major problem. Search as she might, she could not find Wendy's treatment card.

This was vital, because it would contain information on the child's progress, and the particular treatments that she responded best to.

As the minutes zoomed by, Fleur gave up the search. The card was either lost or the qualified had taken it home with her. Either way, it was not here.

Fleur felt a mild panic flutter in her stomach. Although she knew the principles of treatment for cerebral palsied children, and although she had received excellent lectures from her teachers, she had never treated such a child.

If she had been to the Barnes Centre, it would have been a different matter. But now she was faced with her first 'hands on' treatment, and she had no experience and no record of the child's physio.

She would have to muddle through as best she could.

She knew Miss Majors was occupied at the moment. She was supervising some proprioceptive neuro-muscular facilitation (PNF) techniques that a student wanted a try on a hemiplegic patient. There was nothing else for it, she would have to start Wendy's treatment and wing it.

Back in Reception Fleur said, 'If you could please bring Wendy into the little gym now, I'll treat her.'

The father carried the little girl as easily as if he was carrying a floppy rag doll. And in the more secluded area they made Wendy comfortable on a high mat. Then Fleur began to untie one of her shoelaces.

Mr Hitchins, who was kneeling on the high mat, began dejectedly, 'We were going away for a family holiday. . .just to the seaside. But I don't think we'll be able to go now.' His voice broke suddenly.

'What's the problem?' asked Fleur.

'It's a chronic problem with our Wendy. It's got to the stage again when she might have to be hospitalised.'

Fleur could see his eyes misting.

The father continued after a pause, 'All the nurses and doctors are very good. . .but when Wendy has to be an in-patient she can't get as much attention. She always seems to go downhill.'

'But what exactly is the trouble?'

'Wendy's so constipated. . .nothing works. Nothing!'

Fleur found herself saying very importantly, 'Have you tried abdominal massage?'

He looked up hopefully. 'Is that a new treatment? I've never heard of it before.'

'No, it's old. Even the ancient Chinese used massage manipulations.' Fleur recited Miss Majors' classroom lecture as if she had done so many times.

'My wife and I are willing to try *anything*.'

Fleur knew that she couldn't instigate a new treatment on her own, so she explained to Mr Hitchins that she would have to clear it before she could go ahead.

She caught Miss Majors just as she was about to oversee Trevor giving a women's back class. The clinical instructor grinned openly.

'That's an excellent idea of yours, Miss Villiers. Let me come and check the little girl out first, though.'

Mr Hitchins was delighted to be introduced to Miss Majors, and listened attentively to every word.

After a cursory examination when Miss Majors tickled Wendy's tummy, she said, 'Abdominal massage is the definitive treatment here. And Miss Villiers will teach you the technique too, Mr Hitchins.'

The father nodded vigorously.

'And remember these things,' Miss Majors contined. 'Wendy's bladder should be empty before treatment. Never give the massage immediately after a meal, it's really best about one hour before lunch. And you can start with a ten-minute treatment and work up to thirty minutes.'

Mr Hitchins looked a bit perplexed. But Miss Majors smiled encouragingly and said, 'Don't worry, Mr Hitchins, you'll soon get the hang of things.'

The high mat in the little gym wasn't suitable for the massage, so Wendy was carried into the main cubicle region.

Fleur placed one pillow under the little girl's head and two small ones under her knees so that the abdominal wall was relaxed. She positioned Wendy as near to the edge of the plinth as was safe. This was to reduce the strain on her own back.

After exposing the little girl's tummy, she put powder on her hands and began working with slow, deep, rhythmic manipulations.

'I'll demonstrate first,' she told Mr Hitchins, 'then you can have a go later.'

She began stroking obliquely down towards the pelvis, one hand following the other. She made her pressure gradually deeper until she felt Wendy's abdominal wall relax.

Then she started on her massage of the colon. 'When you do the massage, Mr Hitchins, you must stand on the left-hand side of Wendy just as I'm standing. And you begin at the right-hand side of her tummy, and travel along the ascending colon first. Then work along the transverse colon, and lastly the descending colon. If you position yourself in this way, you'll move the contents of the bowel as they would normally.'

'Why must I stand on the left-hand side?' he asked curiously.

'Because if you stand on the wrong side, you're liable to do the manipulations the wrong way round, and you'll actually be forcing the contents of the colon backwards. You'll make Wendy even more constipated!'

'I see,' he laughed. 'I'll do exactly as you say.'

Fleur followed her stroking manipulation with kneading, then finished the work with some relaxing stroking once more.

Mr Hitchins was eager to have a go himself. After a little while he got the idea of relaxing his hands.

When the treatment was over and they had dressed Wendy again, Fleur made another appointment to see the little girl. She felt rather proud about turning what could have been a disaster treatment time into what she hoped would prove a success.

As Fleur waved father and daughter goodbye, a wicked grin crossed her face. Another of her classmates let her borrow her copy of

Gray's Anatomy, and Fleur made her way towards the Rehab canteen.

Very soon the buzz went about the department. It was a stroke of luck that Miss Majors and Trevor were closeted in the big gym. And by teatime, most of the students had made arrangements for their patients to be supervised, and so were able to gather in the canteen.

An air of expectation and excitement had built up in the department. And when Fleur saw the women file out of the gym, she knew Trevor would be along soon.

Shortly he strolled out, looking very pleased with himself.

'I presume you had a favourable debriefing from Miss Majors,' said Fleur. 'Come along for coffee and tell me all about it.'

He fell into step easily by her side. 'Of course, I had a few minor criticisms about my class technique, but I've left the hopeless situation far behind now. She's not a bad old stick really.'

As soon as Trevor entered the canteen he stopped dead in his tracks. 'What's up? Is it somebody's birthday?' he queried.

Several tables had been pushed together and the chairs arranged in a semi-circle. Two chairs remained empty, and on the table in front of them was a bulky object covered by a white tablecloth.

Trevor became wary and began to back away because every single person was staring at him.

'You can't run away now, you great goon!' Fleur caught his elbow. 'It's time for you to act out your part of the wager.'

'What wager? What's all this?'

Trevor tried to make a bolt for the door, but several of the male students collared him and hauled him to his chair. Then the white tablecloth was whipped off and the *Gray's Anatomy* revealed.

While Trevor was being forcibly leaned on to keep him in his seat, Fleur announced, 'I've just given an abdominal massage for constipation on a cerebral palsied child. Eat up!' She pushed the knife and fork towards him.

After much explanation and back-up from the other students, Trevor laughed, throwing his head back.

Then with a sly look he said, 'The joke's on you, Fleur, because you wouldn't take the wager.'

Fleur had anticipated this, and a series of 'I would have taken the wager on if you'd asked me, Trev,' was all the encouragement Trevor needed. He picked up his knife and fork with a flourish and began an imaginary carving action.

Suddenly the canteen was silent. Trevor and Fleur looked up to see Miss Majors. Trevor gulped audibly as the clinical instructor advanced.

Pushing a packet of indigestion tablets on top of the textbook, Miss Majors said, 'I think you might need these, Mr Link.'

By the coolness of her tone and the deadpan expression on her face, nobody knew whether to laugh or not.

However, after an awkward moment's silence, Miss Majors produced a plate from behind her back. 'Or perhaps treacle tart would be more to your liking?' She put the plate on the table in front of Trevor. 'I believe it's your favourite pudding, and that comes as no surprise to me. . .you usually end up in a sticky situation!'

Every student laughed uproariously.

When Miss Majors left, Trevor whispered to Fleur, 'If only that woman were fifty years younger I'd make a pass at her!'

At home that evening Fleur was in high spirits. Not only did she spontaneously burst out laughing when she remembered Trevor and Miss Majors, but there were only three more days before Max's return.

When her father came home that evening he found her in the lounge reading a textbook on vertebral manipulation.

The livid look in his screwed-up eyes put her immediately on the alert, and before she could ask he had whipped out a medical journal from his briefcase.

'Read this, Fleur!'

She sat up rapidly, and her eyes nearly popped out of her head when she saw the letter page.

'You can see your predictions have been totally unfounded,' he began. 'That damned man Buchanan can still find time to continue his character assassination of me.'

'He can't have. . .' Fleur almost choked on her words. Blood rushed to her head. But she had to remain on her guard. She could hardly tell her father that Max had promised there would be no more letters.

She felt weak and sick as she scanned the words. Yes, it was the very letter she had seen on Max's desk all those weeks ago. The deceitful swine had betrayed her!

'It's a damned good job I've entered for the HDH grant,' her father ground out. 'When that piece of research is published, I'll be able to put a stop to that young pup's infernal yapping!'

Anger spurted through Fleur's veins, setting her spirit on fire. 'Yes, you do just that, Dad. Make sure you drag this swine's name through the mud!'

Fleur was so upset, she pleaded a headache and left the room hurriedly.

As she closed the door behind her, she did not see her father's superior, knowing look.

Once in her bedroom she cried hot, bitter tears into her pillow. How could Max have betrayed her? And so swiftly too! His promises and silky words were nothing but a fabric of lies.

Fleur was so hurt that it felt as if a physical pain was swelling within her heart, and it took the best part of an hour for her to stop crying. But as the trickle of tears ceased, her mind became focused on one thing. Revenge!

In the past her strategies and tactics against Max had all failed. She lay quietly contemplating. Timing had been the essential element that had been lacking in her previous plans.

She had two more days before Max returned to England. That would have to be enough. Gradually she began to formulate her plot. And she was sure she could win with the help of her cousin Paul Hogarth.

After her father had retired to bed, Fleur rooted out the *Journal* and found the offending page. The letter that followed Max Buchanan's was on an entirely different subject. It was a short one. And Fleur mentally calculated the number of words. Then, late at night when the moon was half concealed by streaky clouds, she penned her reply.

She revealed her plot the following morning to Ros, while they were changing into their white coats in the students' locker-room.

'From all you've told me about Max, I don't believe he deliberately sent the letter. Someone must have picked it out of the wastepaper basket,' Ros defended.

'I don't care how much you plead his part, I'm going ahead with my plan.'

'It's the most lunatic thing I've ever heard. You'll get yourself into real trouble, Fleur.' Ros sounded exasperated.

'I think I'll be perfectly safe. And I'll have the satisfaction of making Max know exactly what it's like to receive such hurtful letters in public. And I believe my Trojan horse tactic will come up trumps!'

CHAPTER SEVEN

TIME was counting down to Max's return. Fleur had only two days left to create her Trojan horse and plant it in her former lover's house. If all went to plan she would just manage it.

Again, it was Mrs Pippin who opened the front door to Fleur. 'Oh, this is an unexpected visit,' the housekeeper said wonderingly. 'But of course, you must know that Mr Buchanan's away.'

Fleur feigned a look of regret. 'Hello, Mrs Pippin. Yes, I know he's been out of the country for over a month now. But he did say I could borrow any textbook if I needed one.'

'Come in, dear. I know you poor students have to burn the candle at both ends.'

Fleur was anxious to get inside the study and be left alone. But it seemed that Mrs Pippin wanted to talk, and it was only polite to listen.

Mrs Pippin continued, 'The house isn't the same without Mr Buchanan, it's sad without his lovely music. Still. . .' she gave Fleur a confidential look 'He'll be back soon.'

'I know,' Fleur nodded slowly, keeping her eyelashes lowered.

'Pity you weren't here this time yesterday, dear. Mr Buchanan rang then; you could have had a nice chat to him.'

This was something that Fleur hadn't anticipated. It suddenly became very necessary to execute her deed hastily.

The housekeeper was still talking. 'But I expect you two keep in touch.'

'Oh, yes——' Fleur jolted her mind back to the conversation '—we write a lot of letters to each other.'

After a few more exchanges Fleur was free to go into the study. She made straight for the great desk. Sorting quickly through the post, she easily found what she wanted.

She picked up the *Anatomy Journal* and thrust it into her shoulder-bag. Her heart began to pound as she zipped it away. Now for a speedy exit.

But before she could reach the door, the telephone started to ring. It made Fleur halt in her tracks. Turning her head quickly, she stared at the phone as if willing it to stop. But it continued incessantly.

She felt like creeping out of the house, and not even saying goodbye to the housekeeper. But she heard Mrs Pippin answer the extension at the back of the hall.

Silently Fleur opened the study door and listened. Then she sighed with relief as she heard the housekeeper say, 'I'll give Mr

Buchanan your message as soon as he comes back.'

The older woman saw Fleur and said, 'You were quick, dear. How about a cup of tea?'

'That's very kind of you to offer,' Fleur stuttered a little. 'But I'd rather get an early start on my study so that I can bring Mr Buchanan's book back tomorrow.'

Mrs Pippin nodded understandingly. 'I suppose your final exams are very difficult.'

'Yes. We'll have some mocks first,' Fleur explained. 'And we'll have a practical exam on one of our patients. Then the examiners can question us on anything we've learnt.'

'That sounds mighty tough. But then you have to have all your knowledge at your fingertips when you're treating patients.'

Their conversation ended, and Fleur was pleased to discover that Mrs Pippin would be in the house all day tomorrow, so she could bring the 'book' back at any time.

Once outside in Dolphin Road Fleur took the fast bus downtown, and made her way to her cousin's printing business that was situated behind the library.

In the stuffy little room where the machines whirred and beat out a great heat Fleur saw her cousin. 'Hello, Paul!' she exclaimed.

'Hi there, I'll be with you in a minute.' He was feeding some papers into a copying machine. When he had finished he turned

and walked towards her. 'Now where's this
piece of sabotage? It all sounded very mysteri-
ous over the phone.'

'You promised you wouldn't tell anyone.'
She looked at him guardedly.

'Of course not, you made it quite clear this
was family business.'

Fleur pulled out the medical journal still in
its sealed Cellophane wrapper, and Paul slit it
open carefully with a sharp knife.

Fleur found the particular page for Paul and
produced her letter. 'If you could just insert
my letter for this one.' She pointed it out.

Her cousin surveyed the *Journal*, then
lightly fingered the paper. 'It's a piece of luck
that you want your letter inserted on this
centre page. I can easily take the page out and
put my fake one in. It will hardly be notice-
able.' Then he looked pensive.

'Why do you look like that? Is there a problem?'

'The paper's very fine quality. I'm not sure
that I've got something exactly like it, but very
close. . . As long as he isn't looking for a fake,
I don't think your target man will notice.'

'That's excellent,' smiled Fleur.

'Now let me get this straight,' Paul said
seriously. 'You want me to take this letter
out,' he pointed to the short one below Max's,
'and you want me to put your letter in.'

'Exactly.'

'OK, let me read through your effort.' He read aloud.

Sir, I have been following with interest the lively interchange between Professor Villiers and Mr Buchanan in your journal. I would like to point out that Mr Buchanan's comments are seriously misleading. His reasoning is faulted and definitely biased. I am of the opinion that he is motivated by malice and vaulting ambition.
Fleur Villiers

Paul raised his eyebrows. 'Phew! It's a bit harsh.'

'I would have made it harsher if I'd had more space.' Fleur was looking daggers.

Paul's voice dropped to a low tone. 'Are you sure you can't work things out by talking to this man? He's obviously no fool—look at the string of letters after his name.'

'We've tried talking and it hasn't worked.'

Her cousin sighed. 'If I were you I'd steer clear of Buchanan. If I were him I'd feel like putting you over my knee and giving you a good wallop on your bottom.'

'Don't worry, I've no intention of going near the man again,' she assured him.

'I'll print the one for you, Fleur, but no more.'

'One will be enough. Thanks, Paul, you're an angel.'

At twelve noon the following day Fleur
made her way back to Paul's printing shop.
True to his word, he had produced a brilliant
fake. Only if you looked very closely could
you see the difference in the texture of the
centrefold pages.

Fleur nearly danced as she watched her
cousin re-seal the Cellophane envelope. Now
Max's *Journal* looked pristine, and as if it had
just been dropped through the letterbox.

After thanking her cousin, Fleur hurried
over to Dolphin Road. And as luck would
have it, she was able to deposit the *Journal* on
the top of the big desk without any interfer-
ence. So far so good, her undercover escapade
was working to plan.

Fleur was working busily in the Physiotherapy
Department. But she was on tenterhooks,
because she knew that Max had arrived back
in England late last night. She suspected he
would take today off work to recover from his
jet-lag.

Her next patient was Wendy Hitchins. And
immediately she saw father and daughter, she
knew that the abdominal massage had been a
great success.

Mr Hitchins grinned like the Cheshire Cat
as he walked into the treatment cubicle. 'We
can't thank you enough, Miss Villiers,' he

began. 'Wendy's so lively now' The little girl cuddled happily against her father's chest.

'Hello.' Fleur pushed her fingers into the tiny hand and was rewarded by a tight grip.

'There. . .you see, she remembers your touch,' the father continued.

Fleur laughed. 'I'm pleased everything's worked out so well. Now, I think today we'll go through another massage session. Just so that I can check that you're doing all the manipulations correctly.'

As they undressed Wendy and positioned her on the plinth Mr Hitchins said, 'My wife was so overjoyed, she cried. Now we'll be able to go away for a few days to the seaside.'

'That's marvellous,' Fleur agreed.

'Wendy loves the ocean, and she enjoys playing in the sand.'

Secretly Fleur was ecstatic about her success. And it was the quickest cure she had ever performed in physio.

When the session was over, Mr Hitchins presented Fleur with a huge box of chocolates. 'Just a little thank-you,' he said.

Fleur would have liked to have kept Wendy on as her patient. After much discussion with Ros, when she had heard about the Barnes Centre, she felt she could have carried out the Bobath, Rood, and PNF treatments herself. However, the qualified physio was due back, so she made Wendy's next appointment with her.

As Fleur was tidying up the cubicle, Miss Majors appeared and said, 'Mr Buchanan would like to see you in his office straight away. You know where it is, in the Clinical Sciences building, on the fourth floor.'

Fleur felt a sudden blush steal into her cheeks. She hadn't anticipated such an early encounter with Max. 'Is it about a patient?' she asked quaveringly.

'I presume so,' replied the clinical instructor. 'What's your problem? Have you got a patient on a modality?'

'N-no. . .' Fleur stuttered.

'Then go up straight away. We must encourage good relationships with our consultants, Miss Villiers.'

Making her way up through the Clinical Sciences building, Fleur felt her heart beat unsteadily. Would Max have found the *Journal*?

His secretary's office was empty, so she strode straight up to his door and knocked as confidently as she could.

Within seconds Max opened the door and drew her inside. He pulled her close against his body and muttered fervently, 'How are you, sweetheart? I've thought of nothing but you ever since I've been away.'

For all her steely resolve, Fleur found it hard

not to respond to his sensual touch. And it was with a mighty effort that she replied coldly, 'I've been perfectly well.'

He held her away and scanned her face intently. She could see his eyes were drooping with tiredness, and the black circles beneath them displayed his obvious jet-lag.

Then he groaned and walked towards his desk. He held up the sabotaged *Journal* and said, 'I suppose my cold reception is all due to this damned letter?'

'Damned letter is right!' she replied hotly.

He sat down wearily on top of his desk and raked his fingers through his hair. 'You've got to believe me, Fleur. I didn't send it.'

She clenched her teeth and raised her eyebrows.

'I swear to God I dropped the damned thing in the waste paper basket. I can only presume Mrs Bramley. . .ever-efficient as usual. . .picked it up, stuck a stamp on it and posted it.'

Max sighed. 'I've been trying to get hold of her, so that I could give you an explanation, but she's still on a touring holiday, and no one can get hold of her. And she isn't expected home for a couple of days.'

'How typical of you to blame someone else!' Fleur shot back.

Max spoke evenly and with a great weariness. 'I can assure you this whole thing can be sorted out as soon as Mrs Bramley returns.'

'Yes!' Fleur flared. 'I'm sure you can get Mrs Bramley to lie for you. She thinks the sun shines out of you, because you fixed her youngest son's leg. I can distinctly remember that she told me she'd do *anything* for you.'

'Don't jump the gun!' His voice rose sharply. 'I'm dreadfully sorry about any upset that this will bring to your father.'

Fleur was so incensed by this continual façade of lies that she couldn't trust herself to reply. She remained obstinately silent.

After an awkward interlude Max burst out, 'Well, haven't you got anything to say?'

'You'll find my reply in the letter that follows yours in the *Journal*.'

His look of surprise was almost laughable. But with a swift movement he picked up the *Journal*, and Fleur watched as his eyes scanned her reply.

The effect was immediate. She watched as his eyebrows lowered over his eyes.

'"Malice and vaulting ambition"—what in God's name is this, woman!' he thundered. 'How the hell did the editor pass such a piece of libel?' He looked up sharply, his eyes focusing like white light into hers.

He continued in a fury, 'This neat piece of writing on your part will send my standing in the medical circles crashing to the floor.'

'I don't care,' she said hastily. 'You sent the letter when you promised not to. You're the one who's continually hurting my father.'

Max thrust the *Journal* away and advanced rapidly. Catching her forearm just above the wrist, he wrenched her close. 'Your dutiful defence of your father is beyond normal limits,' he ground out. 'And your father can't keep you at home as his little girl for ever. It's about time he let you go. It's about time you grew up and looked at things in an unbiased light!'

'I suppose you'd like me to grow up in your bed!'

'Don't be childish! That's not what I meant. Although I've made no secret in the past that I've wanted you.'

As his temper rose, his grip on her forearm became vicelike.

'Let go, Max!' She tried to jerk her arm away, but it was no good, he held on to her and jerked her back. Once more she tried to free herself, but his strength was superior.

'Stop it!' she cried again. 'You're hurting my elbow!'

'Tantrum elbow. . .' he rasped sarcastically. 'It's a fitting condition for a little girl who won't behave.'

Fleur was incensed by his words. With her free hand she slapped him with all her might full across the face.

He let go immediately.

She rubbed her elbow just above the joint and bit back, 'If this is tantrum elbow, then that is arrogant cheek!'

Now she raced on, 'Your letter to my father was printed so that the whole medical world could read it. But my reply to you is a limited edition of one.'

Max stopped glowering and stared at her openly.

'Yes,' she continued hotly, 'I wanted to hurt you. I wanted you to know just what it's been like for my father to see vicious letters in print.'

He cut in swiftly, 'Are you telling me that this *Journal* is a piece of sabotage?'

'Exactly. And if you could think logically and coherently in a scientific way, Max, you should have known that my reply should have been in next month's *Journal*. There's been no time to send it to the editor for this month's publication.'

He stood still for a moment as if he was stunned but was trying to take in the significance of the whole situation.

Then the thunderous anger in his face subsided, only to be replaced by a calm, cold expression.

'I've underestimated you, Fleur.' He spoke each word deliberately. 'You have the makings of a superb undercover agent. And if this is your game, then I have only one thing to say. . . Play on!'

Fleur was shocked. What exactly did he mean? Now she could feel her blood boiling and searing inside her veins. Inwardly a creeping doubt appeared in her mind. Suddenly she didn't think she was any match for Max. Now all she wanted to do was retreat.

In a weaker voice she said, 'Did you call me up here to talk about a patient?'

A hint of a smile tugged at his lips. 'No,' came the calm reply, 'I wanted to see you, that was all.'

Hastily Fleur excused herself and ran outside. If she thought she would receive great pleasure winning against Max, she was wrong. She had only managed to rile him further.

And what would be his next tactic? Would it involve her father? Or just her? She shuddered at the very thought. Definitely she was out of her depth with this man.

Two days later Fleur was sitting alone in the students' area of the Physio Department, when Max unexpectedly strolled in.

Miss Majors came hurrying to greet her favourite consultant. 'Good afternoon, Mr Buchanan. What can we do for you?'

Arching his neck and making a great play of rubbing his trapezius muscle, he answered,

'I've been operating in theatre for hours. The tension is really building and it's treatening to give me a blinding headache. And I've got a huge clinic this afternoon.'

Fleur's heart plummeted. She stood up stealthily and was about to go and hide in one of the cubicles when Miss Majors called her back.

'Miss Villiers, I see you're doing nothing at the moment. Mr Buchanan needs a soothing neck and shoulders massage—take him into the more secluded area of the department.'

'Yes, of course,' Fleur replied mechanically. Inwardly she could have wept on the spot. Damn the man! This must be one of his retaliation tricks. His timing was impeccable. How the hell did he manage it?

Max was escorted to the rear of the department. As Miss Majors left Max and Fleur in the cubicle she advised, 'Remember, Miss Villiers, be calm and unhurried throughout the massage. This will convey itself to Mr Buchanan and help him to relax.' To Max, she said, 'A twenty-minute session should be sufficient.'

'Excellent,' he said with a subtle note of triumph that wasn't lost on Fleur.

Forced into this intimate situation with Max, Fleur fought to assume a cool detachment. She tried to sound as professional as possible.

'Just slip off your shirt, Mr Buchanan,' she asked him.

'Anything you like,' he replied openly.

'Just your *shirt*,' she emphasised.

She placed an arm table against the wall and piled pillows on top. She noticed that Max removed his white coat, shirt and tie with lightning speed. Nothing much wrong with his neck and shoulder muscles when it came to undressing!

Then she positioned a wooden chair in front of the arm table. 'It will be best if you sit like this, Mr Buchanan, with your forehead resting on your hands.' After giving the demonstration she stood up.

'It'll be a pleasure, Miss Villiers,' he grinned.

Not if I can help it, she thought. Her mind was racing. It was going to be difficult to execute this treatment.

Fleur thought it might be best if she explained the different massage manipulations during the treatment. This way she might be able to keep on top of the situation.

When he was sitting comfortably she began, 'I'll start with effleurage over your trapezii and other lateral muscles.'

'Sounds good,' came the muffled reply.

Fleur started her stroking action from the nape of his neck and progressed to the point of his shoulders. Because the students had practised this technique only recently in the classroom, she knew that the deep stroking produced a wonderful feeling. This she regretted bitterly.

The feel of his well-toned muscles beneath her hands began to have a direct sensual effect. She tried to fight it down. When he had undressed she had caught a glimpse of his magnificent torso and his dark hair emblazoned across his pectorals. But thoughts of his betrayal made her strong.

Shortly she could feel his body relax under her touch, so she decided to progress to a deeper manipulation.

'Now I'll try some kneading. This is a squeezing kneading, and I'm using the whole surface of my hand to squeeze and lift and relax your right upper fibres of trapezius.'

The sigh that escaped the surgeon's lips told Fleur, in no uncertain terms, that he was enjoying himself.

Swiftly she changed to circular kneading, and manipulated the muscles on either side of his spinous processes. She travelled from the nape of his neck downwards.

'What are the effects of this circular kneading?' he asked.

She explained in a detached voice, 'As I press the soft tissues against your underlying bone, it will promote a better blood supply to the muscles. And this will increase nutrition; it also has a sedative effect.'

She was trying hard to sound as clinically professional as possible, but she knew from experience that the massage effect was sensual.

It was coffee-time in the middle of the afternoon, and only a few patients and physio students were left in the area. It was almost as if Fleur and Max were alone.

Max mumbled something, but because his nose and face were pushed into the inverted V of the upper two pillows, Fleur was forced to lean close and ask, 'What exactly did you say, Mr Buchanan?'

'I think this massage is having the *desired* effect.'

Fleur only raised her eyebrows at this. She didn't trust herself to give an answer.

Then as her circular finger kneading progressed further down Max's spine, he started to groan softly. Fleur was embarrassed and annoyed that he should express his pleasure in this way. If anyone else in the department heard, whatever would they think was going on?

Leaning forward, she whispered close to his ear, 'If you don't keep these moans and groans to yourself, I'll put a Chinese firecracker down your trousers!'

Max turned and lifted his flushed face so

that he was looking directly into her eyes. 'I think you've already had a hand in putting it there!'

This did it! Fleur was furious with the direct sexual suggestion. And when she heard Miss Majors call to another student and say that she was going to the gym, Fleur decided that a change of tack was definitely on the cards.

'Put your nose back between the pillows,' she told Max firmly. 'I'm going to move on from the soothing massage. This is a natural progression.'

'Oh. . .good!' He sounded hugely delighted.

'This is a more stimulating massage to improve circulation and improve the tone of your muscles. I think I've achieved all the relaxation.'

Immediately Fleur changed to stimulating stroking. This she performed with excessive vigour, and to her pleasure she heard Max gulp audibly.

Quickly she raced on to hacking, and all the time she described the techniques aloud. 'In hacking I use the ulnar or little finger sides of my hands in a quick slapping motion. . . Now I'm going over your neck muscles. . .and now over your scapular muscles.'

He gave a stifled cough as she increased pace and pressure. The sound of her hacking grew louder as she continued with all her might.

'Now for beating and pounding,' she ground out close to his ear. She gave his upper back a thorough going over for good measure.

'Dear God, woman, do you want to pound the life out of me?' he protested.

'Chest patients on the ward regularly get these treatments, and they never complain.' Fleur felt exuberant to be in control like this.

Unfortunately her treatment time was up, so she finished her session with the stimulating stroking once more.

Suddenly she heard Miss Majors, so she said, 'I think your treatment is over for today, Mr Buchanan. You can get dressed now.' Max's back was very red after the massage and Fleur wanted him covered up before the clinical instructor could see.

Much to her annoyance she heard him laugh into his pillow. It was too late, Miss Majors came into the cubicle. But fortunately Max turned and put on a suitably professional face.

'Now, how's our patient?' Miss Majors began.

'An excellent treatment session,' Max spoke up. 'I've enjoyed every minute. I even feel a new man.'

Fleur gave him a sharp look. He might say anything!

Miss Majors inspected the surgeon's neck and shoulders. 'Miss Villiers has worked up an excellent erythema here. You look quite pink, Mr Buchanan.'

'She's done a very thorough and professional job, Miss Majors, especially with her deep kneading.'

'I'm so glad we've been of service, Mr Buchanan,' the clinical instructor cooed delightedly. 'And any time you feel the need, I'm sure we can accommodate you again.' And off she went.

Fleur would have made her escape quickly too, but Max caught her gently by the elbow and whispered, 'Thanks, Fleur, I really enjoyed the experience. We could continue any time you like at my house.'

'No way! She sounded defiant. 'All I want you to remember is the stimulating massage.'

'Ah. . .yes,' he replied laconically. 'I enjoy nothing better than a *stimulating* woman.'

Fleur cringed inwardly. Max had turned the situation upside down with his remark. Damn him, why did he always win!

CHAPTER EIGHT

EVEN three weeks after the massage incident with Max, Fleur still recoiled at the recollection. Thank goodness all her other patients were sane!

It was directly after lunch and she was rubbing the name of a discharged patient from the board in the department.

'That's a piece of luck.' Fleur swung round to see Miss Majors holding a treatment card. 'I've got a businessman outside who needs a lunchtime appointment. Would you like to treat a Dupuytren's contracture?'

Fleur said eagerly, 'Yes, I'd love to. I've never treated one before.'

'Good. Jim Beacon is one of Mr Buchanan's patients. There are some specific instructions for treatment.' Miss Majors pointed to the front of the card. 'You see, after his time in North America, Mr Buchanan is interested in using some higher therapeutic ultrasound doses. He'd like this patient treated at 1.0 W/cm^2 pulsed.'

'That's high,' Fleur commented.

'Yes. I've examined the man's hand, but I think the skin will tolerate it. But call me periodically so that I can take a look and keep an eye on things.'

Fleur walked out into Reception and called her new patient's name. Jim Beacon was a stocky man of about fifty. He wore a well-cut executive suit that was slightly baggy at the knees.

'Thank you for taking me so quickly.' He was all smiles. 'When you run a company your time isn't your own—this is my lunch hour.'

'It was lucky timing,' Fleur explained. Then she led him into a cubicle.

Here she pulled out a chair and an arm table with a pillow on top. When he had removed his jacket and rolled up his sleeve, she began her examination.

She knew that a Dupuytren's contracture was a contracture of the palmar aponeurosis. Fortunately Jim's condition didn't look as though it had been long-standing. There was a nodule of thickened tissue in his palm and a slight puckering of the skin, but she couldn't see any flexion contractures in the flexor tendons of his ring or little finger.

'I don't know what caused it,' he said, looking steadfastly at his hand.

'It's a tricky condition,' Fleur told him. 'Often people can't pinpoint any injury. But there is a hereditary predisposition.'

But Jim didn't know of anyone else in his family who had the condition.

To get to the deeper facts Fleur had to ask for more details. 'What kind of company do you run?'

'We manufacture and supply fire alarm systems. The company has been in the family for generations.'

'Do you ever work any heavy duty machines? Anything that would cause a vibration into the palm of your hand?'

'No such luck any more,' he sighed. 'Now I'm at the top, all I seem to do is push paper, spend my time in meetings, and troubleshoot.'

Fleur laughed easily with him.

Jim looked serious. 'Mr Buchanan said I must have injured my palmar apon. . .'

'Aponeurosis,' she supplied.

'Yes. What exactly is that?'

'It's a thin but tough membrane. It lies directly under the skin, and runs from the wrist to the near ends of your fingers.'

Fleur asked many more questions and then, 'Is there anything you can do to make your hand feel better?'

'Funny you should say that—only last night I was helping defrost the freezer and I found that after I'd been handling the frozen food this rucked-up part felt easier.'

It was unusual to treat a hand with ice. But,

if Fleur explained to Miss Majors, this treatment could be instigated.

'What are you going to do to make me better?' Jim asked.

'The main treatment will be high-frequency sound waves. You won't hear them because the human ear can't pick them up.'

'Will it hurt?'

'No, not in the least. All you'll feel is a flat piece of metal, the treatment head, moving across your palm.'

When Jim was satisfied with the explanations Fleur went to find Miss Majors, and reported the information about the ice.

Miss Majors considered the matter. 'If the patient feels it helps, then go ahead with wet ice. Dupuytren's is a curious condition, and I'll be interested to see how Jim Beacon responds.'

Having cleared the treatment, Fleur set her patient up for his ice. She placed a plastic sheet and a towel on top of the pillow on the arm table, and positioned a wet towelling bag full of crushed ice under his palm.

'This is just a ten-minute treatment,' she explained. 'But if your hand begins to feel very painful for any reason, then ring this bell.'

When the time was up Fleur dried Jim's hand and applied transmission gel in preparation for the ultrasound. Then she placed the ultrasound head of the machine on Jim's palm. This was the size and shape of a small hand torch, but the head was a plain metal face.

Before switching on the machine she gave Jim the customary warning. 'If you should feel any pain or undue heat during the treatment then tell me immediately.'

After a minute or two, while Fleur moved the treatment head in a steady circular motion, Jim said, 'I can't feel anything at all. How do I know anything's happening?'

Fleur laughed. 'Lots of patients say this. I'll prove the machine is working after the treatment.'

Following the initial five-minute dose, she passed a tissue to Jim so that he could clean off the gel. Then after wiping the head of her machine she said, 'I'm going to get some water and you'll see how the machine works.'

With the water from a plastic cup Fleur sprinkled a few drops so that they covered the treatment head. 'Watch closely now,' she told Jim.

Then she switched the machine to a constant beam, set the intensity high and turned on. The droplets of water began to bubble.

'That's amazing!' exclaimed Jim, his eyes steadily fixed.

As Fleur turned up the intensity the bubbling became more agitated. 'If I turned it way up the water would boil,' she told him.

'Don't upset your machine,' Jim advised. 'You've proved your point, I'm a believer now.'

Next she gave the hand some thumb kneading over the thickened aponeurosis. She used a lanolin-type cream for this because it made the massage easier. Then she performed some passive stretching. This was to make sure that the flexor tendons of his fingers didn't contract. In extreme cases the nail could be forced right down into the palm of the hand.

Afterwards Jim studied his hand. 'I think it feels better, even after one session,' he said.

'Good,' Fleur sounded pleased. 'You'll have twelve treatments, then you'll be reviewed again by Mr Buchanan.'

Pulling on his jacket, Jim said, 'I've just remembered something. My wife bought me a new toothbrush a couple of months ago, and now I think about it, the handle is rather short and it does tend to dig into my palm. Do you think that could have caused it?'

'Ah. . .' Fleur raised her eyebrows, 'that might be very significant. As I said before, the cause of Dupuytren's is generally unknown, but a repeated micro-trauma like that might have started some irritation. And the palm of the hand is very sensitive.'

Jim nodded. 'I'll buy a toothbrush with a

longer handle on my way back to work.
Hmm. . .you all seem very knowledgeable
and efficient here.'

'I'm glad you think so,' smiled Fleur. They
agreed on the day of the next treatment and
Jim left the department.

Fleur was late walking home that evening
because she had stayed for a long time at the
School chatting to Ros. Now, in the blazing
summer heat, some road works forced her to
take a detour down Dolphin Road.

As she approached number sixty-two, she
looked up at the handsome façade. She was
half angry, half sad when she thought of the
master of this house.

Angry because she believed that her father
was literally working himself to death. Unfortunately he had placed all his hopes on winning the HDH research grant, and he spent
long and punishing hours labouring late into
the night. Fleur had even taken the precaution
of looking up first aid treatment for possible
heart attack.

But she was sad too. Deep in her heart she
knew she loved Max. If only he hadn't broken
his promise and sent that last letter to the
Journal. If only Mrs Bramley had retrieved the
letter and sent it by mistake. Then she might
feel free to really love him.

Only yards away from the high hedge that

fronted his house, Fleur began to be wary. She knew he had left the hospital early this afternoon, because he had some free time.

If he saw her now he might well take the opportunity to rush out and play another retaliation prank.

Huh, she wasn't going to fall for any more of his nonsense. If she saw him, she'd say 'Good evening' politely and walk straight past with her head in the air.

Coming level to Max's front drive, she saw some garden tools lying haphazardly on the lawn, and a garden fork leaning at an odd angle, half in the earth.

Then to her horror she saw Max lying in an awkward slumped position. His head was partly under the hedge.

A red alert warning of heart attack flashed across her mind. Instantly she was filled with fear. Heart attack was one of the commonest causes of death for people in the prime of life.

She sped towards the crouching figure and skidded to a halt by his side. Turning him over quickly, she said urgently, 'Max darling, it's all right, I'm here. I'll get you to the hospital as soon as possible!'

Automatically her fingers flew to his jeans belt buckle to loosen his tight clothing. But as she took a closer look at his face *she* was the one in shock.

She had expected his face to be ashen, his

lips blue, and his skin to be sweating profusely. Instead, she saw that his face was a healthy ruddy colour, and that his skin was not clammy but only slightly damp with perspiration. And it was quite obvious that he was breathing and his heart pumping blood.

She turned a brilliant pink and stuttered, 'I. . . I. . .thought. . .'

Max's faculties were firing on all cylinders. Before she knew it, he had pulled her down on to the springy grass and now his weight pinned her there.

Between feverish kisses that covered her eyes, her cheeks and her mouth, he ground out, 'Fleur darling, if you can't wait to rip my clothes off, we'll make love right here!'

She struggled beneath his weight, she was gasping to reply, but his mouth repeatedly covered hers. At last she managed to catch her breath. 'For heaven's sake, Max, I thought you'd had a heart attack, but there's obviously nothing wrong with you. Now get off!'

Her cries were useless. He rasped close to her ear, 'You're wrong, Fleur darling. There is a problem with my heart, and this is the best recovery position I can think of——'

'You fool!' she shot back into his thick hair.

'No, it's true,' he raced on. 'Ever since I've set eyes on you, my heart's been in a flutter. And because you keep refusing me, I've been aching ever since.'

He could barely control the laughter in his voice, and this incensed Fleur even more. After a great deal of pushing and heaving and wriggling, she managed to scramble free and stand up.

She was shaking and breathless, and now she was even more furious with Max because he remained sprawled on the grass. His eyes insolently travelled up the contours of her legs. Immediately she stepped back, and bitterly regretted not wearing trousers.

'Get up, you great malingerer! There's nothing wrong with you, and I don't trust you in that worm's-eye position.'

He laughed outright. Then more seriously, 'I haven't been studying worms. But before you rushed up and pounced on me, I was becoming better acquainted with a black-heart ladybird.'

Fleur groaned and shook her head slowly. 'There's a streak of insanity in your personality!'

Max rummaged beneath the leaves under the hedge. Then he pulled one out gently and placed it in the centre of his palm. Standing up slowly, he pointed to the tiny black and red creature.

'Look, Fleur, this little beauty really does have a black heart. The shape is just above her head.'

Suddenly Fleur was curious, she couldn't resist taking a look.

Max explained, 'The heart shape is really two black spots, but where her wings meet they slightly overlap, and that gives the impression of a single Valentine heart.'

'You're right.' Fleur was enchanted and stared at the little insect.

Max tipped the leaf slightly to one side so that she could get a better view. As he did so, he chuckled softly, 'She's a brave little critter. She's trying to box me with her right front leg and her middle left leg.'

Fleur couldn't help laughing with Max, the situation was so crazy.

After a few more moments Max replaced the ladybird under the hedge. Suddenly Fleur wanted to leave; she was beginning to feel wary again.

And when Max stood up again, he turned and claimed her two hands in his. 'Thank you for coming to my aid like that.' He sounded deadly serious. 'If I had suffered a heart attack, you would have saved my life.'

Looking up into his warm brown eyes, she could feel all her love for him ebbing back. But something in her mind made her distrust him. 'I would have done the same for anyone,' she shrugged.

'Come into the house, Fleur, we have some business to settle.' He slipped his arm around her shoulder and that electric feeling flowed through her once more. She was powerless to refuse and walked with him into his study.

Standing by his desk, he was oddly silent for a moment, as if deliberating something. Then he reached for an object.

'Not another *Journal!*' she exclaimed exasperatedly. 'Don't tell me yours has arrived early and there's another problem!'

As she was raising her eyes to the ceiling she missed the fleeting glint of wickedness in his eyes.

'I'm sorry, Fleur, but there seems to be some more confusion. I'd written a letter to the editor saying that I didn't want to continue the argument in public with your father. However, I've been so tired and so overworked lately that I must have put the wrong letter in the envelope. Here. . . I think you must read this for yourself.'

Fleur was trembling as she took the *Journal*. And when she read on, her legs went weak.

Dearest darling Fleur, Your body drives me wild. Your kisses inflame my passion. Sleep with me tonight, but, as you say, I think it would be best if we kept our affair secret.
Your ever ardent lover,
Big Maxi.

Fleur sank on to the chesterfield. 'Dear God, what will my father say when he reads this!'

Then, looking up at Max, 'You fool! I've never called you Big Maxi in my life!'

'I live in hope.'

Suddenly she came to her senses. There was something of a grin on this man's face. Hurriedly she examined the quality of the paper on the letters page. Ah, yes. . .it was of a slightly inferior quality. But before she could retaliate Max spoke.

'Clever little detective! I see I didn't have you conned for long.'

Fleur flung the *Journal* on the carpet. 'You swine, you've been conniving with my cousin!'

'Yes. It seems the Hogarth press has been working overtime lately. Now, you can hardly be mad with me, Fleur. I've only been following your lead.'

She clenched her teeth. 'What kind of man am I up against?' she spat out.

'The joking stops right here,' he replied with a cool command. 'I've only played you at your game because I could think of no other way of getting through to you. I'm serious about you, I always have been.'

He slid on to the chesterfield by her side. 'Mrs Bramley's back from her holiday now. She's somewhere in the house at the moment. Please come and talk to her, and she'll explain how she picked that letter out of the waste paper basket and sent it by mistake.'

Fleur's mind was whirring with confusion. 'You're capable of the most devious and despicable tricks.' she bit back. 'Mrs Bramley's so loyal, she'd do anything for you. If you want to play Big Maxi with someone, then I suggest you find someone else. I'm sorry I started anything with you!'

She stood up quickly and marched out of the study. And though she could hear him calling her name desperately she did not break her stride.

At the bottom of the front steps, Fleur was greeted by the old housekeeper herself. She was carrying a basket of freshly cut roses over one forearm. But she was wringing her hands in agitation. Her face began to crumple, 'Oh, miss, I couldn't help overhearing you and Mr Buchanan. I'm so sorry for all the upset. It's all my fault. . . I. . .' Here she broke down and began to sob.

Fleur had always thought that Max could put Mrs Bramley up to an Academy award performance. But as the older woman continued to cry she knew that her feelings were genuine.

Mrs Bramley wiped her eyes on her apron. 'It's all to do with that letter that I picked out of the rubbish.'

Now Fleur's heart was in her mouth, as she put an arm around the housekeeper's shoulder. 'Take your time. . .'

'Mr Buchanan's been really mad with me. He is untidy, and I thought the letter had fallen there. So I put the stamp on, and sent it.'

Fleur sighed to herself, she felt so relieved. Max had been telling the truth all along. It had been her prejudice that had made her unable to listen to fact.

After blowing her nose, Mrs Bramley went on, 'Mr Buchanan's been like a bear with a sore head. And the worst part is, he hasn't been playing his lovely music. He's been sitting at his piano banging out horrible discordant sounds.'

Fleur broke in gently, 'Thank you for telling me all this, it's explained a lot. Now, don't worry any more. Go and have a cup of tea or something, while I sort things out with Mr Buchanan.'

Mrs Bramley's wrinkled face broke into a smile. 'You'll go right now, won't you, dear?'

Fleur couldn't help but smile, 'Yes, I'm going to him right now.'

She retraced her steps thoughtfully. The door to the study was still ajar, and she pushed it open silently. Max was leaning against the marble mantelpiece. His figure was a picture of dejection. His arms were outstretched to their fullest extent and he was clasping the marble edge tightly. And his head was pushed up hard against the face of the wooden clock.

Remorse shot through Fleur's veins. She walked up behind him, slid her arms around his waist, and placed her cheek against his back. She felt the tension in his muscles immediately.

'I'm sorry,' she said simply. 'I've just had a word with Mrs Bramley. Now I know that you've been an honourable man all along the line.'

He turned slowly in her arms, then, with his index finger, tipped her chin up. 'Mrs Bramley isn't lying out of some sense of duty to me,' he said seriously.

'I know that now.'

He held her hard against the full length of his body. His kisses were passionate and deeply probing. And Fleur felt the fire spread from his aroused masculinity and flicker like a fire in her veins.

She stood on tiptoe and pulled his head even closer. There was a desperation in their kisses, the long-drawn-out time of quarrelling had fuelled this.

'Come to bed with me now, sweetheart,' he urged.

'Yes, I can't wait much longer either.'

'Are you sure you want me, Fleur?' His dark eyes were dilated and they burned into hers.

'I want you more than anything in the world right now.'

He caught her round the waist, and they almost ran to the study door. But a moment's hesitation in her step made him say, 'You're not having second thoughts, are you?'

Fleur looked at the floor. 'Not second thoughts,' she replied shyly. 'It's just that I'm not on any form of contraception.'

He spoke slowly and very softly. 'Will this be your first *full* experience?'

The excitement was mounting wave upon wave within her body, yet she was embarrassed. 'Yes.'

'I'm sure I've got some condoms upstairs. Don't worry. This first time will be a very special experience for us—I'll make sure of that.' Then, after a slight pause, 'And if you help me put the condom on, we'll get to know each other better.'

The bleeper attached to Max's belt sounded imperiously. 'Not now, for heaven's sake!' he almost exploded. He glared at the object as if he could break it into a thousand pieces.

Then speaking more gently to Fleur, 'I'm so sorry, sweetheart. I'd forgotten I was on call.'

Fleur was mortified, but she knew that, if she wanted to live with this surgeon for the rest of her life, then she had better get used to these summonses.

Max contacted the hospital, and Fleur's

:

greatest fears were realised. After replacing the receiver he explained, 'It's a multiple pile-up on the motorway. They're calling in every available surgeon. It looks as if everyone who can hold a knife will be working right through the night.'

She stroked the tousled hair off her man's forehead. 'I know it's tough. But I understand that you have to go.'

He held her close again. 'At moments like these, I always think. . .what if it was someone that I loved and they were in desperate need of surgery. . . I'd want a surgeon to turn out.'

'I'm very proud of you,' she said earnestly, hugging him tight. 'And I'll be praying for you throughout the night.'

As she disengaged herself from him she said, 'I think you'll have to take a *cold* shower before you go into Theatre!'

'That won't be enough. I think I'll have to lie down in the path of an approaching glacier.'

Fleur had to accept that Max would contact her again when he had the time. Some of the patients might be critical for many days, he didn't know yet.

Although it was a desperate wrench to let him go, she waved him goodbye with a feeling of immense pride.

CHAPTER NINE

FLEUR'S heart was with Max as she headed home. Then she cursed. Her mock final exams started the day after tomorrow, and she had forgotten a textbook on the manipulation of the peripheral joints. So she had to trudge all the way back to the School of Physiotherapy.

Taking a short cut through the hospital, which was busily humming with the present emergency, she found herself behind two surgeons. She couldn't help overhearing their conversation.

'You been called in as well, old boy?'

'Hauled away before I could finish my supper,' replied the other. 'This stint of motorway mayhem will keep us working into the small hours. They've rounded up every surgeon who can hold a scalpel—even the music doctor!'

They both laughed derisively, then hurried towards the lifts.

Fleur was staggered. Inwardly she burned with resentment at the notion that these two general surgeons should denigrate Max. She had worked with Max's patients and seen many examples of his surgery over the months.

Now she and everyone she knew held Max in the highest esteem. His surgical technique was brilliant even with the most difficult cases. She had heard from the theatre staff that he worked painstakingly to achieve the topmost engineering precision.

And he had the gift of establishing immediate rapport with patients. Recently Mrs Jolley had confided that Max reminded her of her beloved husband.

Fleur believed her man's time in the arts had made him a more caring all-round doctor. Again she smouldered at the facetious remark she had overheard.

No wonder Max worked like a Trojan. He was up against this intractable science prejudice.

Back at home Fleur tried hard to concentrate on her study. It was difficult, because her eyes kept wandering to the clock. All the time she was thinking of Max. Sleep was fitful too. Her man was on her mind.

At breakfast the following morning her father said, 'You're looking rather peaky, darling.'

'My mock finals are tomorrow afternoon, remember. I'm feeling a little edgy.'

'I don't know why you worry, you'll sail through.'

'Thanks for the vote of confidence,' she smiled as she spread marmalade on her toast.

Her father's voice was light. 'I've just heard the latest on the research grapevine. My biggest rival for the HDH grant is none other than my old sparring partner, Buchanan!'

Fleur swallowed hard, and her eyes opened wide. 'Are you quite sure?'

'I have my sources in the highest possible places.' He gave her a level look.

For the rest of the morning Fleur's mind revolved around this recent revelation. She was convinced that her father was wrong. Surely Max would have told her?

At coffee-time she had half a mind to page Max, but she heard that he was back in Theatre with a team of surgeons. They were working on a particularly critical case that needed additional surgery.

Shortly afterwards Jim Beacon rang to ask if he could possibly have a morning appointment today. Some overseas consultants were arriving unexpectedly early, but he didn't want to lose his physio treatment.

Fleur juggled her patients and luckily she was able to slot Jim in. And while she was applying the ultrasound Jim spoke appreciatively.

'It's incredible how quickly my hand has responded. I'm not sure what's been the most effective, though—the ultrasound, the massage, the stretching, or the fact that I'm no longer using the short-handled toothbrush that dug in.'

'I should say all have played their part,' Fleur commented. 'Only rigorous scientific research could prove the point specifically. If we had, say, thirty patients all with exactly the same problem, we could give some only ultrasound, some only the massage, and so on.'

'Hmm,' he said, considering, 'medical research must be very difficult. After all, it's not like testing a sheet of metal for its response to fatigue.'

'No,' agreed Fleur. 'And with patients there's always the human factor. Personality can play an important role in recovery.'

After the treatment Miss Majors popped in to see how things were progressing. 'I'm glad I've caught you, Mr Beacon; I've been wondering about this hand.'

The clinical instructor palpated Jim's palm. 'This is excellent,' she enthused. 'I'm sure you're pleased.'

Jim told her, 'I've been impressed with every aspect of my treatment. It's been professional and efficient all along the line. In fact I'd say the NHS is as well run as any private company competing in a world of market forces.'

Miss Majors raised her eyebrows approvingly. 'Just tell everyone you meet that!' Then

turning to Fleur, she asked, 'What dose are
you up to now?'

'1.8 W/cm^2 for eight minutes.'

The older woman nodded. 'Mr Buchanan's
North American treatment ideas seem to be
working out splendidly.'

When the treatment was finished Fleur
reminded Jim that he had agreed to be a model
for her mock practical exams tomorrow. He
checked it in his diary and assured her that
he'd be present.

After lunch in the canteen she had twenty
minutes to spare. Ros and Trev went back to
the School to brush up on their study. But
Fleur was desperate to see Max.

She wanted to know all about his night of
surgery. And that matter of the HDH grant
niggled at the back of her mind.

Fleur knocked expectantly at Max's office
door.

'Come in.'

She was delighted that her lover was here,
even if his voice did sound tired.

'I didn't expect to see you so soon, sweetheart.' He put down his dictaphone and held
his arms out wide. In an instant she was in his
strong arms. He flicked his white coat aside
and pulled her on to his lap.

He kissed her deeply, then sighed content-
edly as he held her face close to his.

'Let me look at you,' said Fleur, inching

back so that she could look at his face. 'You're exhausted. I bet you didn't get any sleep last night.' She rubbed her thumb pads gently beneath his puffy red eyes.

'I was lucky, I managed to snatch a couple of hours' sleep at four this morning. There were some spare rooms in Residence.'

'And was the time in Theatre very bad?'

'Bad enough,' he replied slowly, his eyebrows narrowing together. 'Some patients are critical, but I don't think anyone will need any more immediate surgery.'

He looked steadfastly into her blue eyes. 'Let me relax for a few minutes with you now, Fleur. You're the best medicine any surgeon could ever need.'

He kissed her again and slid his hand under the fullness of her breast. She felt her skin tingle to his touch.

Lifting his lips from hers, he said, 'I've got to lecture in ten minutes—not enough time to work my woman up and satisfy her.'

Fleur giggled.

'Tell me what you were doing last night.'

'Oh, studying, because I've got my mocks tomorrow afternoon.'

'Are these the ones where you'll be examined while treating a patient?'

'Yes. Jim Beacon has very kindly agreed to model for me. And by the way, his hand is coming on terrifically.' Fleur explained about the treatment methods.

Max nodded approvingly. And when she told him about the change in toothbrush, he looked directly in her eyes and clicked his tongue.

'That's my clever little detective! You do excellently on the medical detection trail.'

Fleur was filled with pride at this praise. She wished she could stay longer locked like this in her man's arms. But time was pressing on, and the problem of the HDH grant surfaced in her mind.

'Is it true that you've entered for the HDH research money?' she asked.

'Yes,' he replied absently. 'I sent in my research proposal months ago, before I even met you.'

Fleur felt a beat of alarm in her heart. 'And are you proposing to study the foot?'

'Yes,' he sighed. 'That same old problem again.'

Cautiously she continued, 'My father has entered for that grant too.'

Shrugging his shoulders, Max said, 'And may the best man win.'

This lack of concern piqued Fleur a little. She'd better handle the situation carefully. 'I can never thank you enough, now you've stopped sending those letters in the *Journal*.'

Max seemed unconcerned with the present

conversation. He was gently brushing his thumb across her erect nipple. Although Fleur thrilled to his touch, she found his actions irritating considering the magnitude of the problem that she was about to open up.

'If my father loses the research grant to you, he'll be so depressed I don't know what might happen,' she sighed.

Max spoke laconically. 'If he wins the research grant, then so be it. And if I win, well. . .' he sighed, 'I don't think I could do better than have your father assist me on the project.'

Fleur flared at the idea. Although Max had provided a solution quite honestly, Fleur did not see it in that light.

'How can you say such a thing! My father would be humiliated after your public wrangle in the *Journal*.'

Max stopped caressing her breast, but he kept his grip firm. 'Don't be ridiculous,' he replied offhandedly. 'And having someone like your father working with me would give my career a much-needed boost.'

'Your career! Is that all you can think of?' She was too hasty in her reply. 'Is my father's health of no concern to you?' she raced on. 'Couldn't you possibly consider withdrawing your proposal so that he has a good chance?'

The flash of anger in Max's eyes immediately put Fleur on her guard.

'Understand this,' he replied with super-soft command. 'I may have stopped the letters, but I will not withdraw from this grant. And you, delicious young madam that you are, will not manipulate my career in any way.'

Fleur bit her lower lip in an effort to keep silent. The old row between them was boiling up yet again.

Max sighed wearily. 'Your father's outstanding academic record and his brilliant works will stand him in good stead. I can't imagine that he won't find any work once he retires from the University. Anyway. . .' he sounded exhausted now '. . .research should be above all this bickering. The good of humanity is at stake. And surely that should be the driving force behind all medical advances.'

His refusal to listen to reason, and the authoritative note in his voice inflamed her. She struggled free from his embrace and replied haughtily, 'Keep your advances, medical and otherwise, to yourself!'

As soon as she was in front of his office door she regretted her outburst. She was on edge because of the secrecy of their relationship, and her mock exams; and Max was obviously drained of all energy after his hectic night in surgery.

She was about to apologise when a loud

knock on the door heralded the entrance of the most senior orthopaedic surgeon in the district.

'Hello, Max. Have you got a minute or two——?' Then, seeing Fleur, 'I'm sorry. I can come back later if you'd like.'

'No, please come in, sir.' Max had regained some of his composure. 'Miss Villiers was only consulting me about a patient.' Turning coolly to Fleur, he continued, 'Thanks. I'll keep all those facts in mind.'

Fleur left after a polite goodbye, which she found very difficult. But there was something headstrong in her nature, and although she felt the quarrel should be patched up soon, she decided to let Max make the first move.

But if Max made any attempt to contact Fleur, she knew nothing about it. And on the day of the exams she was so nervous that she pushed Max right out of her mind.

All the patients, except those who had agreed to act as models, had been cancelled for the day. Fleur and Ros would be the last candidates to be examined, and that would be in the late afternoon.

Not wanting to study alone any longer, Fleur made her way to the hospital Rehab canteen, and had lunch with Ros. Afterwards they sat in one of the deserted practical classrooms and tried to forecast the possible questions.

The door to the classroom opened suddenly. 'Here you are at last, Miss Villiers! I've been out of my mind trying to contact you.' The deputy head walked towards them briskly. Fleur felt a moment's panic.

'Now, there's no need for you to be upset. Everything's going to work out. Miss Majors has received a phone call from your patient Mr Beacon. It seems he's stuck in London and he can't make it for your practicals. He's terribly sorry.'

'No patient?' Fleur blurted out. 'Is my exam going to be cancelled?'

'No. Miss Majors thinks the sustained stress would be bad for you. She's worked something of a miracle for you, though.'

Fleur wondered which of her patients Miss Majors had been able to haul in at such short notice.

The deputy head continued, 'Pete Lowe, a rheumatoid patient, has kindly volunteered. I believe you've treated him before.'

'Where did she find Pete?' Fleur was amazed. She had been swotting up the hand, and orthopaedic conditions related to trauma.

'Miss Majors found him in a rheumatoid clinic. She organised lunch for him on one of the wards, and now he says he's only too delighted to help.'

The shock made Fleur turn two shades paler than her best laundered white coat.

'Now, don't worry. All this will be taken into account in the exam,' soothed the deputy head. 'And Mr Cutlord, the orthopaedic surgeon helping us examine today, is a real sweetie.'

When the teacher left the classroom, Fleur felt like bursting into tears. But Ros came to the rescue. 'Don't panic, Fleur. I'll refresh your mind with everything there is to know about rheumatoid arthritis. And she's right, these highly unusual circumstances will be taken into account.'

Feeling faintly sick, Fleur thanked her friend, then listened to all the information. But all too soon it was time for Ros to leave for her own exam.

'Good luck,' said Fleur.

'Thanks. And after my stint, I'm going to stick around here until you come out. I'll want to hear all the details.'

They wished each other luck again, and Fleur was left alone to steady her nerves.

After combing her hair and checking that her white coat was immaculate Fleur made her way to the department and was ushered into the secluded traction area that had been reserved for the exams.

She saw Pete already on the plinth with his leg in elevation. He was prepared for his Jobst.

Looking very relaxed, he gave her a friendly wave which she returned.

Miss Majors suddenly hurried up. She had a look of concern on her face. 'Now, Miss Villiers, there's no need to panic further.'

What was this all about? Fleur's heart was pounding enough already.

The clinical instructor went on, 'It looks as though you're in for another surprise. Unfortunately Mr Cutlord has had to dash away on a family problem. But, thank heavens, I've managed to line up another surgeon to examine you.'

'Who?' asked Fleur innocently. All the surgeons were fairly easygoing, and she didn't really mind which one she had.

'Mr Buchanan has agreed to save the day.'

This shock was so great, Fleur felt as if her mouth would literally fall open. She could hardly think straight. Why in heaven's name had she quarrelled with Max about the research grant? Why hadn't she rung him and apologised?

Now the continuing controversy dangled above her head. And Max was about to examine her on a patient with a *foot* problem! No doubt he'd take every advantage of this. The exam was going to be like the Spanish Inquisition.

'As it will be a few more minutes before Mr

Buchanan arrives, set Pete up on his Jobst now,' advised Miss Majors.

While Fleur was positioning the Tubigauze on Pete's foot he said, 'Buck up, you're the last candidate today, and the examiners will breeze through. They'll want to get off home early.'

'It wouldn't be so bad,' she whispered, 'but the usual surgeon who examines has had to leave. Now I'm stuck with someone new.'

'Don't fret now, it can't be bad. And if you dig into one of my sensitive spots while you're doing the massage, I won't say a thing. I'll grit my teeth and bear it.'

'Thanks,' Fleur smiled. 'I'm sure I couldn't have a more helpful model.'

The minutes ticked by agonisingly slowly, and still Max hadn't appeared. So Miss Majors advised Fleur to remove the Jobst and start the massage.

Immediately Fleur's hands were covered in cream Max arrived. He looked formally severe yet handsome in his starched white coat. Yet the expression on his face was inscrutable.

'I apologise for keeping everyone waiting,' he began.

'It's good of you to come,' Miss Majors beamed, then made the introductions.

Pete held out his hand eagerly, and Max placed his large hand gently in the patient's. Fleur noticed that he did not squeeze or pump during the handshake. Although the joints in Pete's hand were no longer inflamed, he might still find it painful if Max inadvertently squeezed a tender spot.

Because Pete's foot was elevated and therefore high in the air, Fleur was standing on a stool to execute the massage. Apart from the embarrassment of their meeting following their last row, she felt faintly ridiculous because the stool made her a few inches taller than the surgeon.

'What massage stroke are you performing now?' Max began his examination.

'Effleurage, sir. A stroking manipulation towards the heart.'

Max scrutinised the ankle. 'I presume you're doing this to remove the slight œdema around the ankle?'

Pete's ankle was much improved since this course of treatment, but some residual swelling remained.

'Yes,' answered Fleur. 'I've started the massage at the proximal end of the leg, and then I'll concentrate on the foot and ankle.'

Now it was Miss Majors' turn to ask a question, 'What are the contra-indications for this type of massage?'

These were reasonably easy questions. Fleur didn't feel too bad. 'Massage would be contra-indicated if Pete had any sort of rash, or any breakdown of his skin with infection. Also I wouldn't give the treatment if he had varicose veins.'

Miss Majors nodded approvingly.

Max turned to Pete. 'Do you find this treatment helpful?' he asked

Pete spoke up enthusiastically. 'The massage is the best part.'

'I know what you mean.' There was a slight lilt in Max's voice. 'I've been fortunate enough to receive a treatment myself. Even though massage is an old treatment, and there are, shall I say, dubious connections in some people's minds, I found it very effective.'

Fleur gulped. She hoped there weren't going to be any more innuendoes like this throughout the exam. Miss Majors only looked well satisfied.

More formally, Max asked, 'Could you tell us the general types of medication used in rheumatoid arthritis?'

Fleur concentrated for a moment. 'Anti-inflammatory, analgesic, disease-suppressive, and cortico-steroid.'

'Give an example of when a cortico-steriod injection would be useful.'

She had to think a moment. 'If a patient has had rheumatoid arthritis for many years, and it's generally burned itself out, but only one or two joints remain active, then an intra-articular injection would be helpful. This would be to prevent persistent inflammatory activity. But it wouldn't be used if the joint had symptomatic destructive changes.'

Thank goodness Ros had coached her before the exam!

Max nodded. But even when Fleur looked into his face, she couldn't tell if she was giving a good impression or not.

The surgeon went on, 'Let's say the ankle joint was involved. Could you point out exactly where the needle would be inserted? Correct technique is vital if you want to avoid further damage.'

Physios don't give injections, thought Fleur. But here we go! We've started on the foot. I'll be for it now. Taking a second to compose herself, she said, 'You could inject on either side of the extensor hallucis longus and the tibialis anterior tendons at the level of the medial malleolus.' She pointed it out.

'Good,' he answered slowly. Then to her surprise he changed tack. 'And if the shoulder joint was a problem, could you point out the site too?'

Miss Majors helped Pete unbutton his shirt and expose the joint.

After wiping her hands on the towel under her patient's leg, Fleur climbed down from her stool and came around to the head of the plinth.

'The best approach would be from the anterior aspect.' Gently she pushed her finger on to the spot. 'The needle would be inserted between the coracoid process and the head of the humerus.'

'And how deep would you expect the joint space to be?'

'At least two to three centimetres.'

Max continued to ask applied anatomy questions that ranged over the whole body. And Fleur was grateful that he didn't return to the foot, or that vexing point of contention, the standing posture.

Max turned to Miss Majors. 'I think that's all I want to ask with the patient present.'

'Fine,' replied the clinical instructor. 'We'll continue our examination at the desk.' She thanked Pete for his co-operation, and said someone would be along shortly to help him down from the plinth.

As they left the cubicle, Pete motioned Max back. Then he whispered low in the surgeon's ear. Fleur couldn't catch the remark, but she saw Max raise one eyebrow and heard him say, 'That sounds just like Miss Villiers!'

Fleur presumed that Pete had said something positive in order to help her. But later, as she took up her chair in front of the desk where Miss Majors and Max sat, she wasn't sure. Max's expression was enigmatic.

Even though Fleur had dried her hands on the towel, she could feel her palms were moist with stress again.

Fortunately Miss Majors asked simple questions relating to the principles of physiotherapy. But Max's questions were altogether different. They were probing, exhaustive and positively relentless.

Fleur answered as best she could. But it seemed that as soon as she had given an answer on one topic, he switched to another.

Finally he asked, 'Can you tell me anything about the influence of disturbed sleep physiology on morning symptoms in patients with rheumatoid arthritis?'

Here was a gift. Miss Majors looked smug. And Fleur, remembering her instructor's little lecture on Pete, trotted out all the information quite confidently.

Max stared at her for some seconds, then, turning to Miss Majors, said, 'I think that concludes my part of the examination.'

'Mine too. Thank you, Miss Villiers. We'll let you know.'

Fleur thanked her examiners, then gratefully stood up. Then after a few sedate paces she almost bolted from the exam area.

She was in such a state of nerves by now that she knew her cheeks were flaming red. So she headed for the washbasin in the progressive resisted weight area. Mercifully there was no one about, and she was able to splash cold water on her face.

While she leaned on the washbasin and

steadied her breathing she was unaware of a sudden activity in the department.

Max ran out of the main entrance door, his white coat flapping. And Miss Majors was not far behind. But outside the doors she stood still, scanning the route back to the Physio School. Then abruptly she returned to the main desk and made a hurried phone call.

Some time later, Fleur dried her face on a paper towel and sauntered out of the department. She wanted to hear about Ros's exam too.

But Ros saw her coming and ran up to her. 'You look terribly dazed, Fleur. I'm sorry about the news.'

'Yes, Max as an examiner just about put the tin lid on today.'

Ros looked alarmed. 'You mean you don't know about your father——?'

'What about him?' Fleur halted in her tracks.

Ros spoke gently. 'Prepare yourself. He fell off the ladder in the library, and he's broken his collarbone. I don't think it's too bad.'

Fleur was stunned into silence. Ros slid her arm about her friend's waist. 'I'll come with you to Emergency,' she said.

They both ran off.

CHAPTER TEN

'I'M SORRY, Fleur, it was a stupid thing to do.
I fell on my outstretched hand.'

She saw her father pale with shock. He was
lying back on the pillows of the examination
couch in Emergency, and he was hugging his
arm close to his side.

'Don't blame yourself,' she said softly.
'These things happen.' Then, coming to the
critical point, 'How badly is it broken?'

'My surgeon's conferring with his col-
leagues at the moment. But I feel the clavicle
will need a bit of surgery.'

Fleur's heart plummeted. 'And who's looking after you?'

He raised his eyes to the ceiling, as if
resigned to some quirk of fate.

Then to Fleur's astonishment it was Max
who entered the cubicle. He greeted her with
a reassuring smile.

'I've got your films here, sir.' Max slotted
them into a viewer. 'The general consensus is
that I should go ahead and operate.'

Professor Villiers craned his neck and
screwed up his eyes to see the X-rays. 'It's a
rare complication. But I agree, those sharp

spurs of bone could endanger the subclavian vessels.'

Fleur felt numb. She knew that if the arteries were affected, then the blood supply to the arm could be at risk.

'I don't think you need have any qualms from the surgical point of view,' Max continued. 'The best theatre staff are standing by. And I'll insert a slender pin through the medulla of the outer fragment of your clavicle, then I'll drive it in a retrograde direction through the medulla and fix it to the medial fragment.'

Professor Villiers started to look concerned as Max went on, 'I'll expose the bone with only minimal stripping of soft tissues, so that your blood supply will be preserved.'

Fleur thought she had never seen her father so frail-looking.

'I can see you're right, Buchanan,' Professor Villiers agreed reluctantly. 'I haven't forgotten that Sir Robert Peel, who established our police force, died of a fractured clavicle. Some splinters of bone ruptured his subclavian vein.'

Then with a look of challenge in his eyes, the Professor added, 'I'm donating my body to medical science after my death. So if you do a botched job many hundreds of medical students will learn all about it when I'm on the dissecting table!'

'For goodness' sake, Dad!' Fleur burst out. 'There's no need for this attitude.' She believed it was generally accepted that children could show you up, but on this occasion a parent was behaving just as badly.

Max replied calmly and graciously, 'When you die, sir—and I don't expect that will be for a very long time—the dissecting students will see what a fine surgeon I've been.'

One up for Max! Fleur was relieved that her father had been suitably silenced. But really, the situation was beyond a joke.

It was agreed that Professor Villiers should spend a few nights in hospital following the operation. And so Fleur went home to pick up some nightwear and toiletries. When she returned to the hospital she faced a long wait before her father was out of surgery.

Finally her father returned, and Max, still in his theatre greens, spoke to her in the ward sister's office.

'The whole procedure went very smoothly,' he explained. 'Here you can see the check X-ray with the pin in place.'

Fleur scrutinised the film. 'The pin's perfectly positioned,' she sighed. 'I knew you'd do a brilliant piece of surgery.'

'It's up to your father to recover now,' Max went on gently. Then, putting his hand on her shoulder, 'You look drained, Fleur. Where are you staying?'

In all the confusion Ros had taken over, and Fleur had let her. 'I'm going to stay with a physio friend,' Fleur told him.

'That's a splendid idea.' His words sounded genuine. 'I'm going to stick around the hospital tonight. If you need me for anything, just page me.'

To Fleur's relief, her father made a good recovery and two mornings later, when she arrived on the ward, he looked in the pink of health.

Five minutes later when Max arrived, her father suddenly turned sulky. After a formal greeting he began without preamble, 'My secretary bought some unwelcome post last night. I presume I should congratulate you on winning the HDH grant.'

'I thought you'd won that, sir,' said Max, a look of astonishment in his eyes.

'Well, if we didn't get the money, who the hell did?'

Fleur chipped in, 'I know—Ros's husband found out last night. It's gone to a sociologist, and he'll be researching into the effects of long-term waiting lists for hospital patients.'

'I never heard such rubbish!' exploded the Professor.

'Give me strength!' Max ground out. 'Why the hell should anyone waste any money researching *that* topic? All they have to do is ask any one of my patients who are unfortunate enough to be kept waiting.'

Inwardly Fleur had to chuckle. This was the only time she imagined her father and Max agreeing on anything to do with research.

Now the two of them seemed to be getting on fairly well on the surface. But Fleur knew her father, and she sensed that he still distrusted Max Buchanan.

If only they could work together on some project. Then the problem of her father's retirement would be solved. And because of Professor Villiers' stature in the academic world, no one would dare denigrate Max by calling him the 'music doctor'.

It would also solve the problem closest to Fleur's heart. If her father worked with Max, surely he would come to know and respect him. And then he would give their love affair his blessing.

Directly after lunch Fleur was called to the phone on the main reception desk in Physio. There was a problem with transport and one of her patients.

Looking pensive, and carrying a huge bunch of white chrysanthemums, Jim Beacon sat on one of the long benches waiting for his appointment. Occasionally his glance drifted to the young patient sitting by his side.

It was Mikey Lockett, the lad of twelve. As it was another boiling hot afternoon, he wore

only flimsy shorts and a T-shirt. The Milwaukee brace that held his whole spine in a rigid
but correct posture was clearly evident for all
to see.

Mikey didn't appear to have a care in the
world. He was leaning back on the bench,
oblivious to everything except his rock music,
which he was listening to under his Walkman
headphones.

As he had his eyes closed he did not see
Ros walk up. She lifted one ear-piece and
called very loudly, 'Anyone in there?'

Bursting into fits of giggles, he greeted her
and jumped up agilely. As patient and physio
made their way towards the treatment cubicles, Jim's eyes were riveted on the pair.

When Fleur had finished talking to her
patient on the phone, she went to collect Jim.

'Hello, I've brought these as a peace-offer-
ing, Miss Villiers.' He thrust the flowers into
her hands. 'I'm so sorry I wasn't able to make
it for your mock exams. I tried my best, but
the situation was beyond my control.'

'Don't give it a second thought. Thank you,
these flowers are just gorgeous.'

'But how did you get on in your exams?'
asked Jim.

Fleur pushed her face into the big round
blooms, then said, raising her head, 'Miss
Majors found another patient. I don't think
the exam was too bad; we have to wait for our

marks to be posted. Students at other hospitals are still being examined.'

During the ultrasound Jim sounded a little tentative as he brought up the next subject. 'I was sitting by a young lad in Reception. I couldn't help noticing that he wore a great cumbersome brace. It was almost like scaffolding running from his hips right up to his chin.'

'That's our Mikey,' Fleur laughed. 'Was he disturbing you. He's usually into some sort of mischief.'

'Not at all. He seems such a happy, well-balanced chap. I was quite struck by his attitude. It was as if he wasn't self-conscious or embarrassed about the brace.'

Fleur nodded. 'That's him. He's got that "look 'em in the eye", and "accept me as I am" attitude.'

Jim continued, 'Even though there was nothing much wrong with my hand, I used to stick it in my pocket to hide it.'

'Many people feel that way,' Fleur reassured her patient. 'It's quite usual.'

'Has the lad a problem with his back?'

Fleur felt a little uneasy. It was unprofessional to discuss one patient with another, so she gave her answer in general terms. 'The brace is the Milwaukee brace. It's used for many conditions of the spine. But the general idea is to keep the back in a straight good posture, until the patient has stopped growing.'

'So he wears it in the day, and takes it off at night.'

'No,' Fleur explained. 'He has to wear it all the time except when he's swimming and when he takes a bath. The brace is literally screwed into position with screws and a screwdriver.'

Jim sounded grave. 'And the lad must wear that thing until he's stopped growing, until he's a man?'

'Yes—it's a tall order. And not everyone accepts the brace.'

'What happens then?'

'If the spine is too crooked, then the patient may have to have an extensive operation and have a strut or a metal rod positioned alongside the bones.'

Jim remained silent for a while. 'Is any research being done at the moment?' he asked.

Fleur explained that funds were notoriously short at present, and that a condition like Mikey's was not well known and therefore was unlikely to attract money.

'I think young people like Mikey could get the attention they deserve, Miss Villiers.'

She looked up from her treatment curiously.

Jim continued excitedly, 'My great-aunt Winifred died recently. She's left a considerable fortune. I'm one of the executors of her will, and she wished that a substantial sum should go for research. But she made the proviso that it should go to children who had to have great courage.'

Looking Fleur straight in the eyes, he asked, 'Do you know any gifted doctors who would undertake such research?'

Her heart began to swell with expectation. Here was the answer to all the haggling between her father and Max. 'Yes, I think I know two brilliant minds who would work on the project, and they would fit your great-aunt's wishes exactly.'

At coffee-time Fleur bounded up the hospital stairs towards her father's ward. And outside his door she heard two voices. Typically, the Professor and Max were having an argument on anatomy.

'No, I simply can't accept your views, Buchanan.' Her father sounded adamant. 'Consider the position of the toes when women wear stiletto-heeled shoes——'

Fleur broke in as if she'd heard nothing. 'Hello, everyone. And how's the patient?'

Max grinned. 'I'm very pleased with his shoulder. And as for the Professor's mind. . .it's in fine sparring form too.'

'Great!' enthused Fleur. 'And I've got some wonderful news. There's another research grant up for grabs. Do you think you two could work together on it?'

'Poof!' Her father raised his good hand and let it drop on to the bedclothes. 'I can't imagine it. Buchanan and I have such directly opposing views, I can't see it happening.'

Max spoke up. 'It's a pity, but I think it would take us a month of Sundays to agree on the hypothesis.'

Fleur was annoyed that they should dismiss the idea. 'Just forget the foot!' She spoke more sharply than she had intended. Her emotions were threatening to get the better of her.

She sped on, 'Why can't you two accept that there's probably no single "correct" posture? As far as I can see, an individual's posture is the best adaption to his different bodily structures. Some stand like penguins, other like pigeons, and some have such bowed legs that they could have had a horse between their legs all their lives!'

On she went. 'Anyway, this research is to do with kyphoscoliosis.'

'Ah, the spine,' interrupted her father. 'That's a complex area. . .perhaps the most challenging of all.'

Max looked contemplative. 'Of course, the position of the pelvis is the keystone to the general body posture——'

'No, no,' her father interrupted.

'For goodness' sake!' burst out Fleur. 'Can't

you two put your brilliant minds together, rather than constantly bickering? You're both from the same mould. Both proud and arrogant. If anyone's to believe evolution, then mankind is one up from the apes.' She took a deep breath. 'But when I listen to you gibbering, the whole situation is nothing more than monkey business!'

The two men turned to her and spoke in unison.

'How dare you speak to Buchanan like that?'

'How dare you speak to your father like that?'

Her father ordered, 'Apologise at once!'

Now Fleur had gone this far she wouldn't give way. 'I'd like to, but I can't under the circumstances. I love both of you, but the idea of making a choice is tearing me apart. No, I can't apologise—as far as I'm concerned the apes are superior. And I won't slander them!'

She was at boiling point. She couldn't trust herself further. So she fled from the room. She felt like bursting into tears, but she still had patients to treat.

After work, Fleur walked home with her head bowed. As she rounded a corner she unexpectedly saw Max. His car was parked by the kerb, and the passenger door was open.

He walked forward and blocked her path. 'Chauffeur, madam?'

She was too tired and weary for any more

confrontation. 'What jiggery-pokery have you got in mind now?' she demanded.

He chuckled softly. 'I like your choice of words, but I have something more serious to discuss.'

'It's not my father, is it. . .?'

'No, he's perfectly fine now.'

She slid into the front seat and waited curiously.

Max spoke earnestly. 'Your father has asked to be discharged tonight. He's arranged to convalesce with your aunt Betty.'

'This is all news to me,' Fleur sounded perplexed. 'What's it all about?'

'It's all about two proud and arrogant men coming to their senses. But only with the intervention of a fairy godmother called Desirée. . .a silver-haired, elegant lady. She's made your father and me see sense.'

'I don't know anyone called Desirée.' Fleur was becoming more confused.

'Yes, you know Miss Majors. And *she* seemed to know the situation all too well. She gave us two boys a good talking to, and the upshot is that we've seen the light. Your father and I are going to submit a research proposal for Jim Beacon's money. And, best of all, your father has given us his blessing.'

Fleur sat speechless, staring into his brilliant, warm brown eyes. It was unbelievable.

All the impossible problems vanished in a twinkling, as if banished by a fairy wand.

And in that instant big tears welled up in her eyes and started to trickle down her cheeks. Max pulled her close and brushed the teardrops lightly away with his fingertips.

'I'm crying because I'm so happy,' she said at last.

Kissing her wet eyes, he spoke gently. 'You've had a hell of a lot to put up with lately. First the wrangle in the *Journal*, then this accident, and your mocks. And you know, you got Distinction in that practical.'

'That's brilliant,' she smiled.

'And Pete thinks you're wonderful too. He whispered to me that you'd saved his sex life.'

Fleur sighed and shook her head. 'All I did was tell Ros, and she organised everything.'

'Perhaps, but Pete said he was too embarrassed to ask outright, but you managed to pick up the problem.'

Max withdrew slightly and reaching into his breast pocket pulled out a small leather presentation box. Fleur gasped as he revealed the sparkling ring.

'What a fabulous ruby, and it's surrounded by diamonds!'

'Yes, I chose it because it reminded me of the black-heart ladybird, and the time you might have saved my life. Wear it, and say you'll be my wife for ever.'

Gently she eased the ring from its box, and Max helped her slip it on. 'Yes. . .oh, yes,' she breathed. 'I've never wanted any man the way I want you.'

He kissed her deeply and she clung to him. Then lifting his head he said breathlessly, 'For the sake of my sexual sanity, will you come home to Dolphin Road now, so that we can get more intimately acquainted in the master bedroom?'

'Home, Max,' she giggled. 'But *do* spare the horsepower. We don't want to have an accident before we get there!'

The master bedroom was upstairs at the front of the house. Two large windows looked out on to the leaves of an ash tree.

Max led her towards the king-sized bed. From his bedside table he picked up an object. Fleur was astonished.

'It's my St George and the dragon sketch that I was working on during your first lecture! And it's framed now.'

'Of course,' he said with a glint in his eye. 'Ever since I first saw you, I knew I wanted you. I knew you'd always be the princess in my heart.'

After replacing the picture, he pulled the ribbon from her hair and let her locks cascade free. Then he undressed her slowly and reverently. She could feel his fingers trembling as he unzipped her dress and eased her slip from her shoulders.

When she was naked he lifted her on to the bed. Her whole body was tingling with excitement, and she longed for him to satisfy her.

With an effort he stood up and announced formally, 'For every great occasion a man should dress correctly. Now, Fleur, what shall I wear to make love to you?'

Her face fell. What sort of a madman had she agreed to marry?

He appeared to stroll nonchalantly towards a Japanese screen that was positioned in front of a fitted wardrobe. And to her disbelief he disappeared behind the screen and started to throw clothes over it.

'Now, sweetheart, I need your advice. . .shall I wear my grey flannel suit, my evening suit. . .' There was a pause. 'Or my birthday suit?'

She burst out laughing, and half covered her eyes with her fingers. 'Many happy returns!' she called.

He poked his head round the screen. 'I hoped you'd say that.'

Then he disappeared again and she could hear him rapidly pulling off his clothes. He emerged from behind the screen and walked towards her, and the full magnificence of his nudity awed her. He was power and strength and beauty rolled into one.

She spoke softly. 'Whoever tailored that suit made a perfect fit.'

Max chuckled mischievously. 'Let's be serious now, Fleur. Let's take our time; it would be so easy for me to take you in a burst of frenzy.' He bent over her and brushed his lips softly against hers.

Delicately she traced the contours of his face. 'I never thought of you as the type of man who's all technique and testicles.'

He roared with laughter, then slid on to the bed and pulled her hard against the full length of his body. He moulded his chest and belly and thighs to her.

He was wonderfully warm, and the heat of his potent manhood pressed firmly up against her belly filled her with longing and desire.

Kissing her softly, he nuzzled her breasts. Skilfully and still with tenderness he delighted every inch of her body, and she experienced thrill upon thrill under his touch.

All the while, his eyes were brilliant and loving.

Max took his time to rouse her and give her exquisite pleasure. She was aware of his fingers trembling as he stroked and quickened her responses to fever pitch, his face a study in masterful control.

She quivered and gasped at the soft touch of his manhood, seeming to awaken her deepest desires. And she gasped at his entry.

She felt as if they were melting together, their bodies and hearts fusing. She clung to him as the waves of sensuality mounted, and when he could finally hold back no more, she accepted the pain of his first ecstasy inside her.

And when at last he withdrew, she felt as if she was losing something precious, for Max had given her a beyond-earth pleasure. And she wished he had stayed with her longer.

They lay breathless and silent in each other's arms, as sweat from their bodies trickled between them. When he had regained his breath, he looked dreamily into her eyes. 'Thank you, Fleur, you're more wonderful than I'd ever dreamed.'

Moments later he screwed up his eyes and groaned. 'Sorry, sweetheart, I forgot the condom.'

'It's much too late now,' she answered, laughing softly. 'And don't be sorry. . . I love big Maxi just the way he is.'

He grinned, then kissed her face reverently.

They made love and slept many times throughout the night. And when the dawn broke through, red and glorious. Fleur snuggled close to her man and smiled to herself.

She knew that researching the romance and sexuality in her man would take a lifetime. And she was going to enjoy every moment.

ESPECIALLY FOR YOU ON MOTHER'S DAY

OUT OF THE STORM - Catherine George
BATTLE FOR LOVE - Stephanie Howard
GOODBYE DELANEY - Kay Gregory
DEEP WATER - Marjorie Lewty

Four unique love stories beautifully packaged, a
wonderful gift for Mother's Day - or why not treat yourself!

Published: February 1992   Price: £6.40

Next month's Romances

Each month, you can chose from a world of variety in romance with Mills & Boon. These are the new titles to look out for next month.

ONCE BITTEN, TWICE SHY ROBYN DONALD
SAVING GRACE CAROLE MORTIMER
AN UNLIKELY ROMANCE BETTY NEELS
STORMY VOYAGE SALLY WENTWORTH
A TIME FOR LOVE AMANDA BROWNING
INTANGIBLE DREAM PATRICIA WILSON
IMAGES OF DESIRE ANNE BEAUMONT
OFFER ME A RAINBOW NATALIE FOX
TROUBLE SHOOTER DIANA HAMILTON
A ROMAN MARRIAGE STEPHANIE HOWARD
DANGEROUS COMPANY KAY GREGORY
DECEITFUL LOVER HELEN BROOKS
FOR LOVE OR POWER ROSALIE HENAGHAN
DISTANT SHADOWS ALISON YORK
FLORENTINE SPRING CHARLOTTE LAMB

STARSIGN
HUNTER'S HAREM ELEANOR REES